MARLENE

# MARLENE

Philippe Djian

*Translated from the French*
*by Mark Polizzotti*

OTHER PRESS
NEW YORK

Originally published in French as *Marlène* in 2017 by Éditions Gallimard, Paris
Copyright © Philippe Djian and Éditions Gallimard, 2017
Translation copyright © Mark Polizzotti, 2020

*Production editor: Yvonne E. Cárdenas*
*Text designer: Jennifer Daddio / Bookmark Design & Media Inc.*
*This book was set in Fournier and Helvetica Neue by*
*Alpha Design & Composition of Pittsfield, NH.*

1  3  5  7  9  10  8  6  4  2

Library of Congress Cataloging-in-Publication Data

Names: Djian, Philippe, 1949- author. | Polizzotti, Mark, translator.
Title: Marlene : a novel / Philippe Djian ; translated from the French by Mark Polizzotti.
Other titles: Marlène. English
Description: New York : Other Press, [2020]
Identifiers: LCCN 2020000353 (print) | LCCN 2020000354 (ebook) |
ISBN 9781590519875 (paperback) | ISBN 9781590519882 (ebook)
Classification: LCC PQ2664.J5 M37 2020 (print) | LCC PQ2664.J5 (ebook) |
DDC 843/.914—dc23
LC record available at https://lccn.loc.gov/2020000353
LC ebook record available at https://lccn.loc.gov/2020000354

FOR

Année

# GIRL

It wasn't the smartest thing to do. It might even worsen
the situation, which wasn't great to begin with. But since
she refused to let him in or hear him out, he rammed
open the door with his shoulder.

Dan hovered a moment on the threshold, weary, about
to give up. She raised her head and gave him a blank
stare—he could have been just anyone, just anything.
The heat wasn't on and the air in the room was frigid.

Listen, he said. Come eat something. Let me think
about it.

She swiveled in her chair to face the window, scraps of
melting ice sliding down it.

Mona, I'm talking to you, he said to her back.

He hadn't taken the time to change and he considered
the mark his footsteps left on the floor, the imprint of his
wet soles on the pale wood. He winced—that kind of
detail bothered him. He danced from foot to foot for a
moment, then retreated without another word.

# BREAK

Nath sighed: her daughter was driving her bonkers. She
no longer knew what to do with her; she felt as if she'd
tried everything and had run out of steam.

He remained silent at the other end of the line. He knew all this.

Dan, I need a break, she moaned.

Outside, darkness was falling, and lights had gone on inside the surrounding houses. He was stuck. Fine, he said eventually. But you'd better be careful.

You're not in my shoes.

I'm just saying.

## OMEN

He glanced at Mona, who had fallen asleep in a chair. Putting her up, even for a few days, wasn't his idea of a fun time. That temper of hers. He was very fond of her, but at a distance, and definitely not from morning till night. He'd already battered in a door, and she had only just arrived. That wasn't a good omen. If her mother was throwing in the towel, what was *he* supposed to do—he who knew nothing and had no desire to know anything about an eighteen-year-old girl whose head and heart were like a vat of boiling sulfur. His back wasn't broad enough for this. It was just broad enough to take care of himself. And even then, only on condition that nothing upset the order he'd worked so hard to establish.

A storm had broken out overnight. Nothing special— lawns torn up, trees knocked down, roofs damaged, alarms, firemen, TV, power outages, etc.—but he could have done without this extra worry. Even at rest, immobile, now quietly asleep and harmless, Mona didn't promise anything good.

He went out to get some air. It wasn't too chilly; the wind had all but died down and the sky was again stretched smooth like a black satin sheet. They'd cleared away the main debris that had been blocking the road—though not blocking it enough, rotten luck, to keep Mona from arriving at his doorstep as he was sweeping away the sawdust from an old fallen tamarisk he'd cut up. The tart aroma of freshly sawed wood and sap lingered in the night air. Broken glass sparkled all around, and several figures, silent and resigned, were still cleaning up in the twilight, slowly dragging man-gled refuse to the curb. He watched for a moment. It seemed appropriate to offer his help. People appreciated that kind of gesture. Having a guy like that as your neighbor. Not very chatty, but always ready to lend a hand. And well built, to boot. And who minded his own business, rarer still.

## BROW

Nath was dressed to kill. Dan had rattled her a bit with his warnings, but she had zero intention of heed-ing them. She glanced at her watch. She felt feverish.

Apprehension, guilt, excitement. The whole goddam circus. She poured herself a drink and tried to remain calmly seated while waiting for it to be time.

She wondered how the two of them had managed to live together even this long, by what masterstroke or dark miracle. Calling her own mother a whore. And so coldly, so contemptuously. Sweet Jesus, who did her daughter think she was.

She shook it off, pinched her cheeks to give them a rosy blush, and hopped in a cab.

And she hadn't even slept with this guy. Not that she didn't want to, but that's how it was. She wasn't a whore. She was just a woman on her own, and that tended to drive her a little crazy at times. But about that, of course, Mona didn't give a flip.

He hadn't realized she was married. He knit his brow. He seemed nice, not terribly bright. My husband works on an oil rig, she told him. We don't see each other much. She shrugged. Let's talk about something else, she said with a smile. He was in insurance. Okay, she said, never mind. Let's go dancing.

He propped himself up on one elbow and knit his brow again as she got dressed. He was young. It occurred to her that the girl he'd someday marry would have a very simple life.

# PRESENCE

Dan set his alarm for four in the morning, but he always
woke up earlier and started his exercise routine while
listening to the radio, then went running for several
miles without ever varying his route, keeping count
of his steps. After that, his day could begin. He could
attack the housework.

His inability to sleep more than a few hours a night no
longer bothered him. He had other worries. The moment he had opened his eyes, this time, and strained
his ears in the dark, his usual reflex, he had immediately sensed the difference. Nothing betrayed Mona's
presence in the house, but one thing he could still rely
on was the instinct he'd developed, the indispens-
able vigilance, the faculty of perceiving an invisible
presence in the sector, even in an ocean of silence and
shadow. He hadn't dreamed. He remained upright in
bed for a few minutes—whereas normally he leaped to
his feet—sitting cross-legged, forehead damp, taking
the measure of this new lousy annoying disturbing
situation.

When she appeared, much later, at the kitchen doorway,
in sweats, barefoot, sleepy, he had just returned from
shopping and was putting away the groceries.

What's that noise I heard in the middle of the night, she
said, yawning.

She meant the rowing machine, the back-and-forth of the saddle and the rhythmic wheeze of the fan blade each time he tugged on the oars and sucked in air.

Oh, yeah, right, she said. Guess I'll have to get used to it.

He paused in front of the open fridge, grimacing to himself.

He washed his hands again as she sat down at the kitchen table for lunch.

I thought you said you'd be there, she said. *Anytime, anywhere.* What was that supposed to mean.

He set a cup and the coffeepot in front of her.

Your mother doesn't have an easy life. Let her work it out with your dad, don't get mixed up in it.

She reached toward the coffeepot. I didn't expect to be welcomed with open arms, she sighed, but even so. Shit, coming from you, that's cold.

He turned toward the window, beyond which lay a pale, uncertain sky. He waited for her to get up so he could clear the table and wipe the Formica, whose perfect brilliance drew a smile of satisfaction from him.

There was still one thing he knew how to do—which had gotten him through more than one desperate situation—and that was make a quick decision.

# HALF

In the space of several months, Richard had put on weight again, his outline had thickened, but he didn't give a damn. Never mind about my waistline, he smirked, crushing Dan in his arms like a brute.

They sat down at a small, austere table, facing each other amid the noise of the room.

I always gain a few pounds in winter, he said.

In warm weather, he melted. Without abstaining from fat, or sugar, or alcohol, which pissed off more than a few people and turned girls' heads as soon as the sun came out. At thirty-seven, he still led the pack with his handsome bad boy looks. That thought comforted him as he gazed after Dan, while the latter went through the door and headed with furtive steps down the hall. If he had to choose, he'd rather be in his own shoes than in that guy's. Be half alive rather than half dead. A matter of temperament.

Richard rubbed his chin for a moment, thinking of Mona and the falling-out she'd had with her mother. He'd deal with that all in good time. At least they hadn't demolished the place. If only these little spats were as bad as things got in life. Nothing to make yourself sick over. Dan wanted everything to be clear, no misunderstandings. There weren't any. There couldn't be. Mona was Richard's daughter. That fucking Dan, he mused,

shaking his head. He stood up with a smile and went
about his business.

## LIGHTNING

If Nath had hoped to enjoy a moment's peace, take
advantage of there being no Mona (who really could get
her goat), it didn't work out that way. She should have
figured as much. She wasn't twenty anymore, nothing should have surprised her. She finished grooming
Scotty—a white, belligerent toy poodle—with clenched
teeth, then pulled on an anorak and went out for a
smoke.
She crossed the parking lot to stand in the sun and
think, but thinking got her nowhere. Marlene was coming. She was almost here. And being in the sun didn't
get her anywhere either, as the east wind was biting
and she felt no warmth, no softness caressing her face.
At times, life seemed like nothing more than that, light
without effect, a dead reflection, a trap, a sick joke. You
always got screwed.
Wait till you meet her, she said.
Dan was no picnic either, in his way, but at least she
didn't have to live with him.
I'm cursed, I swear, she continued.
Dan studied the pictures in an album she'd opened for
him. He'd heard about Marlene but had never met her

in the flesh. Nath never brought her up. In fact, he'd almost forgotten she had a sister. In a photo of the two of them at age twenty, Marlene was the one wearing glasses.

While Nath was already sexy, luminous, and supple as a young stem, Marlene was stiff and dull, as if a black cloud had maliciously settled above her head.

That's the long and short of it, said Nath.

Outside, the sun was at its zenith.

You see, she went on, if Marlene were here, sitting where you are, it would be raining buckets. It's not a nice thing to say. She's my sister. But some people are like that. Some people just attract lightning, or I don't know, whatever calamity is nearby. I don't need that. Especially now.

Dan buried his nose in the mug of black coffee that was getting cold at the edge of the table. Nath liked it strong, put in three times the normal amount. Enough to give you palpitations.

She waited for Dan to leave before going to lie down a minute, then headed back to the salon to shampoo those miserable mutts who bared their fangs at her. She had to take advantage of every instant of calm she had left before that evening, when she'd go pick up Marlene at the station.

# RAVIOLI

On the way, Dan stopped at the bank to deposit his pension check. It was a good time of day, there wasn't much of a line—in garrison towns, most guys were overdrawn and preferred to make themselves scarce, hide out in the corner bar rather than hover wistfully around the tellers' windows. He had known times like that, and still skirted the precipice when he occasionally went off the rails. He withdrew some cash, sent his mother a money order, and spent the afternoon at the bowling alley—maintaining the pinsetters, oiling the lanes, and so forth, three times a week—and when he got home after dark, Mona declared she was famished. He'd forgotten all about her and had grabbed a sandwich.

You shouldn't have waited, he said.

Couldn't find the can opener.

He pulled a hunting knife from one of the kitchen drawers and showed her how not to starve to death with a can of beef ravioli.

Watching her eat, he imagined her doing a survival exercise in enemy territory.

What's so funny, she asked.

He shook his head with a satisfied smile, appreciating that she'd asked the question without undue hostility. Mona wasn't of a piece. Neither was the world. Besides, it was often in the evening, before he sank into the somber murk of his nightmares, that a ray of light filtered through and he felt he just might return to the surface.

You've got a healthy appetite, he said.

She shook her head with her mouth full. Then, pushing away her plate, she announced, I'm not sticking around this shithole forever. And as he didn't answer, she added, I'll see how it goes.

He remained silent. He was glad she wasn't his daughter: he wouldn't have to fret about her. All the same, she sure was ballsy.

## CLIPPERS

Richard had gotten three months, but so what. That wouldn't keep him from doing it again. They could lock him up as much as they liked. It made no diff, being shut up on the inside or the outside. Whether sitting still or driving like a maniac, the thrill was the same. The intoxication never subsided, and never had. With or without alcohol. With or without speed. The world flew by.

But that's how it was in this country. That's how they thanked you.

He raised his eyes to the guy shaving his head.

I'm getting out in three weeks, he said. Hold it for me till then.

The guy turned off the clippers. Yeah, but I've got somebody, he winced. That's kind of a problem, know what I mean.

Richard turned and looked at the man over his shoulder.

All right, fine, said the other. I'll hold it for you. Don't have a cow.

Richard closed his eyes. All in all, he was anxious to get out.

## MIST

Dan wasn't curious, or was no longer curious, which amounted to the same thing. He wasn't especially interested in knowing what she looked like and was in no rush to meet her. But Nath had called early that morning, just as he was noticing Mona's hair in the shower drain and glaring at it in annoyance. Can you come, she'd asked. She hung up before he could answer.

Well, we're off to a good start, she said, cursing at the zipper of her windbreaker. She's lost the key to her baggage locker.

What do you mean, lost.

How should I know, ask her. I'm in a rush.

She left, slamming the door behind her in a whirlwind of snowflakes. He took the opportunity to wash his hands. With pale pink liquid soap, not entirely to his taste. Pressing on the dispenser pump, Dan accidentally sent a spurt straight to his chest. He stood there a second, nonplussed.

I did that too, said a voice behind him. Stupid piece of junk.

Marlene was wearing the same glasses as in the photo. During the day, she wore contacts, but they were packed away in the suitcase she had to retrieve from the station. Actually, she alternated. She hadn't counted on snow. She didn't know the area. She hoped she'd like it here, that Nath would take the time to show her around. She couldn't understand how she'd managed to misplace that goddam key. She was sorry to bother him with this nonsense. It's very kind of you. It's really awfully nice of you, she said. It looks like a quiet little town, she said, wiping the mist off the windows. Quiet is important.

He slowed down, pointing out the main shops while trying to avoid looking at her. The snow never lasts very long around here, he said. In a few hours, it'll pretty much be gone.

He handed her off to a station employee he knew, an old regular at the bowling alley—the guy had an impressive record for making some really tough splits—and he killed time in the cafeteria with a white beer while Marlene dealt with her key problem.

Outside, the sky was clearing. He lowered his eyes to the still viscous soap stain forming a halo on his sweatshirt. He touched it with his fingertip. It was gummy and made a faint unpleasant sucking sound. He forced himself to think about something else. That woman, Marlene—she seemed kind of flaky.

When she reappeared, visibly relieved, she handed him a partially eaten bag of fries. I know, I shouldn't, she said with a shrug.

There was a suitcase and a travel trunk. She looked around for a cart, but he grabbed the trunk with one hand, the suitcase with the other, and she gazed after him for a moment with a blank face while he headed briskly toward the exit.


## RESTROOM

Picking up a 7-10 split wasn't an everyday thing. To knock off the two pins left standing, the two farthest apart, is practically a miracle. Professional players only manage it about once in a hundred and fifty tries— diddly-squat. Dan had finished his workday and was watching a player at the edge of the lane scratching his head and making a face.

Night was falling. Dan always had a drink at the bar before going home. The music wasn't great and the atmosphere was pretty noisy—the smack of bowling balls, pins flying in all directions, the hubbub of voices—but it was his haven of peace, his no-man's land, his sensory deprivation tank. Sometimes a guy would ask him how's it going or a woman would climb onto the stool next to him, but he had a knack for keeping people at bay— exchanging a few brief words now and then was the limit of his sociability.

Nath knew this. She knew all she needed to know. Which didn't keep her from saddling him with Marlene, not troubled for a second about yanking away his one moment of relaxation and calm. It wouldn't kill him, according to her. Not only wouldn't it kill him, it would do him good.

What are you talking about, he'd answered. I don't even know her. What are we supposed to say to each other. You're really something.

Oh, come on, be a pal. Just do this little thing for me.

I'm putting her in a cab. I have to go now.

Wait, don't hang up.

It was no use, she already had. Then Marlene had appeared, and now she still wasn't back from the restroom. After a good ten minutes. It was a long time. He tried using it to think of something they might do, but no ideas came to him, not the least inspiration; his mind was spinning on empty, a complete blank. He no longer knew what it meant to take a woman out. The fellow who was getting ready to try his 7-10 split also seemed short of ideas.

Dan waited for him to make up his mind—to blow it by sending his ball into the gutter—before standing up to see what was going on with Marlene.

He hesitated at the door of the women's restroom and made sure no one was watching before he entered. Inside hovered a sickly sweet aroma, of cheap quality and tepidly floral, in a faux-cozy decor, with sinks shaped like scallop shells. Having called her name a few times to no avail, he pulled himself up to glance over the door of the stall and saw Marlene sitting on the toilet, inert, slumped against the wall like a rag doll, eyes closed, glasses askew, a few sheets of pale pink toilet paper still in her hand.

That was all he needed to see: he dropped back to his feet and undid the lock with his passkey. She opened her eyes, gave him a distraught stare, her skin ashen. Not moving a hair, cheek crushed against the wallpaper, neck twisted, panties around her knees. Without a word, he leaned over and scooped her up, lifting her from the bowl and taking her out of the stall.

She couldn't stand; her legs wouldn't hold. It was as if her bones were made of rubber. He rested her as best he could against the row of sinks and quickly pulled up her panties while averting his gaze.

For a moment, he had to hold her close to keep her from crumpling to the floor. He swore between his teeth, then noticed she was coming out of her fog.

Oh. Oh, forgive me. I'm so sorry, she finally stammered.

It's nothing, he said in a dark voice, immediately moving away from her. No harm done.

Marlene claimed the evening had gone well. She added with a distant smile, well but nothing more. Nath remained puzzled for a moment, holding the coffeepot, while her sister sat at the table in the sun-drenched kitchen. I wouldn't exactly call him a chatterbox, Marlene continued, then expressed her delight in the beautiful day outside.

Conversation isn't their strong suit, Nath sighed, shaking her head. Just gotta make do. Richard's no better. She felt slightly bad about ditching Marlene the day after her arrival, but she had no regrets. She'd gotten what she desired. She wouldn't burn in hell for it.

To make it up, and because she felt more relaxed, lighter than the day before, she took Marlene for a drive around the area, from the precisely delineated residential suburb to the wooded hills, still covered in snow, just north of the city; then to the reservoir where people went swimming in summer, the army base, passing by the shopping center, the drive-in movie theater, the disco, the service stations; after which came a long stretch without relief or vegetation, just a wide, straight road that seemed to go on forever.

You have to enjoy small-town life, Nath said as she braked in the bowling alley parking lot. Have to not mind being bored.

She glanced at her sister as they headed for the entrance and thought to herself that the battle wasn't over yet. Night was falling and the giant tenpins on the lit rooftop sign were already blinking in the misty twilight.

They sat at the bar. This wasn't the Ritz or the Carlton, the few guys standing at the counter left them alone, but Nath, watching Marlene squirm on her stool, immediately recognized the neurotic, edgy, semi-adrift girl she'd had for a sister and had lugged around like a millstone all childhood long.

Cut that out, she hissed. Everything's fine.

Marlene let out a small apologetic giggle and tried to sit still.

You should get new glasses, Nath advised her. Seriously.


## GLASSES

Dan didn't know much about that. He didn't have an opinion. Seriously. Instead, he was concerned about the two women's plan to drop in on Mona unannounced, which they wouldn't let go of. They'd had a drink or two before he joined them and their eyes shone a little too bright.

I just can't wait to see her, Marlene repeated for the nth time.

He grimaced. He got up to fetch some beers—might as well, at this point. He was tempted to just take off and let them fend for themselves.

Who's that girl with Nath, asked a veteran at the bar. Her sister.

Huh, whaddya know, didn't know she had a sister.

Dan nodded, gathered up the beers, and returned to their table.

I don't want a war, stated Nath. She's an adult now, after all.

I don't have any advice to offer. I'm not going to come between the two of you.

I'm sure it'll work out, Marlene announced. We can all make a fresh start.

They stared at her without saying a word. Outside the bay windows, a cold moon was rising in the sky. Guys in fatigues and regulation haircuts were horsing around and laughing in the parking lot. Cars were finding spots.

Did I say something wrong, asked Marlene.

Dan, on his motorcycle, arrived a few minutes before the two women, with a worried face but a fresh complexion, intent on warning Mona that she was in for a surprise—if that could soften the blow.

Lights were on in the living room and kitchen windows. He scowled. He hoped everything would soon return to normal.

She was taking a bath. Hence that candy smell that had indelibly permeated the place for the last few days and put him ill at ease. He announced the two women's visit through the door. No response. He heard the tap running.

At that same instant, a huge crash froze his blood and took his breath away. It came from outside. He faltered, seized by one of those flashes of panic that sometimes grabbed hold of him. He flattened against the wall, jaw trembling.

Still, just as he was about to lose it, he recognized Marlene's voice exclaiming oh my god, oh Jesus, oh shit.

He opened his eyes, swallowed. He gave himself a moment, bit into his fist, and mopped his damp brow. Then he went outside, legs still shaky, to see what the ruckus was about.

Marlene had driven into his motorcycle. She hadn't just hit it, she'd sent it flying against the garage door, which had suffered its own damage. She had an explanation for all this, it seemed, but he wasn't listening and walked over to pick up his bike.

I'm so sorry, I'm so so sorry, she wailed at his back.

He grimaced, and at the same time realized Nath was nowhere to be seen.

Oh, she changed her mind at the last minute, Marlene said. I dropped her off at her place. If only I'd known.

She seemed truly sorry. Sozzled, but sorry.

Where was my brain, she went on.

He gave her a dark look, then turned back to his mauled vehicle and the garage door that ballooned inward like a reverse paunch. Costly as it was, at least there wouldn't be a huge blowout between mother and daughter. Not tonight, at any rate. Not here. Who knew what might have happened.

He looked up at the black sky, noted the artificial calm hovering over everything. Marlene was carefully inspecting the car's bumper, hunting for scratches. He asked where her glasses were.

This'll make you laugh, she said.

But he wasn't to have that pleasure, for she stopped short when Mona appeared in the doorway.

## REARVIEW

On the way back, Marlene, slightly tipsy and sans glasses, wore a vague smile about her lips. She hadn't been able to see her niece grow up, but she was still feeling the rush of hugging her tight. A real temperament, and a real beauty; a smart girl, though visibly suffering the rigidity of adolescence—especially when it came to her mother. Stopped at a light, in the center of town where things were hopping around bars with flashing neons, she tapped her fingers on the wheel and glanced at herself in the rearview mirror. She thought about Dan, what an odd duck he was. Then she concentrated on her driving and didn't give him another thought.

To spare herself an unpleasant comment from her sister, she made no mention of the unfortunate little incident that had occurred as she was pulling up to Dan's house and instead put the accent on the wonderful time the three of them had had.

Nath scowled and said she was going to bed.

She made an about-face when Marlene announced point-blank that she was pregnant. I'd like to talk to you about it, she added.

## CREEPS

It didn't show. It didn't show *yet*. Observing Marlene from behind, in the bathroom mirror, all the while brushing her teeth with unusual ardor as her sister straddled the edge of the tan thermoformed acrylic bathtub, Nath pondered whether she shouldn't take advantage of the situation and drown her once and for all.

Don't be too long, she told her. We've got a lot to do.

It was beautiful out, a bright March sky in absolute, strident blue. In front of the kitchen window, pensive, Nath put cream on her face. The Italian coffeepot belched. Richard was under lock and key, Mona had slammed the door on her way out, Marlene had dropped into her lap like a bag of cement, and as for the rest, as for her love and sex life, the Lord had not exactly provided. The only thing missing was crummy weather.

The world was full of creeps. Nath had been all about finding some guys to teach the bastard who'd tossed

Marlene out on the street when she got pregnant a lesson. At least, make it so he'd never do it again. But Marlene had gone all timid, Miss Above-It-All, and flatly rejected any sort of punishment. Nath had shaken her head. Christ almighty, I really don't understand you. Her sister was no picnic, but that hardly justified it. They stopped at the bowling alley to retrieve her glasses, after a morose, silent ride, each lost in her thoughts—so close in space, but so far apart in reality. The woman who'd found them had sat on them and broken one of the temples—a major tragedy, to hear Marlene tell it, as she tried in vain to adjust them on her nose, whining that she didn't have the resources just now to take on the cost of repairing them, nor in fact to take on any expense at all.

Don't tell me you're broke, Nath sighed, looking for a place to sit.

I've been meaning to talk to you about that, went Marlene.

## FLASHES

Richard would have to settle a nice, plump debt the minute he set foot on the outside. He had no particular fondness for Italian models, but Alfa Romeo was a name that spoke to him—that murmured in his ear before settling into the basso profundo of a V6 with exhaust

23

cutout. Naturally, he'd have to tweak it, soup up the engine, accessorize with a direct air intake, sixteen-inch tires, etc., and all of that carried a price tag. So it was important not to antagonize Nath. Not start shouting. Until he could replenish—and his three months in stir had bled him dry, financially speaking—he'd have to play it cool, show tolerance and patient composure.

After all, she's your sister, he said, touching her hand.

She stared at him fixedly for a moment. Most men were such lousy actors. Transparent. But on the other hand, she had opened an account for Marlene and loaned her enough for a month. Something that, under normal circumstances, Richard would have found difficult to swallow.

She pulled away her hand in confusion.

Anyway, it's just a loan, she hastened to add. I'm taking her on at the shop.

Nath, that's for you to decide, he said with a smile. Family is family.

It'll be all right. She'll make out.

Yeah, he eluded. Let's hope she doesn't start sleeping around all over town.

Seeing that she didn't appreciate the remark, he added, Never mind, forget I said anything.

He had a hard time feeling sorry for Marlene, compassion not being his strong suit. He had very little in reserve, to be dispensed with a dropper. Saving any for Marlene, that nutcase whom he'd met maybe two or

three times at most, who went into a tailspin at the drop
of a hat and attracted shit like a magnet attracts iron,
was a waste.

By the end of the visit, and although she had remained
quietly seated across from him like a schoolmarm,
talking stuff and nonsense, he had a hard-on like a mule.
He would have paid a fortune for the two of them to be
left alone for a minute. The days were long gone when
he came home from a mission, half-crazed, still hallu-
cinating, a bundle of nerves, and when he kept fucking
and fucking Nath, moaning with pleasure in her arms
like a child, for days on end. All that was long gone. But
there were still flashes, heat lightning, an irresistible
yearning for her despite the truckloads of young women
who were always around, who turned up in droves, who
moved in with their husbands and their brats, among
whom he could pick and choose; all those adorable little
bitches that he, somehow, deserved—he figured he had
fought hard enough for them, for his country, for God
knows what, and even for those asswipes who had given
him three months for speeding, repeat offender or no.
He grimaced as his eyes met Nath's, who stood up to
leave. Repeat offender, my ass, he thought.

Welcoming guys home from a stay in hell was a duty, a tradition, a time for emotions, hugs, and tears as families reunited in the station lobby decked out for the occasion.

Night was falling, the train was running late, and noses and cheeks were reddening in the cold air that flowed under the glass roof, where a large welcome banner flapped, made from a PVC tarpaulin that they dug out each time—Dan and Richard had had their turn with it a few years earlier, coming back from Afghanistan, and you could bet it would be used again.

The veterans were supposed to set an example, and unless they had moved away, or were in the psych ward or behind bars, they were expected to be there to lend the event the necessary decorum, and Dan had just noticed that Marlene had new glasses—she was walking toward him, waving broadly—when the train headlights pierced the darkness in the distance and a noise of joyful relief rose from the crowd.

She kissed him on both cheeks, which took him by surprise and irritated him more than anything else. If he could avoid being seen with her, so much the better. He stood stiffly, arms hanging limp, so that she felt a moment's hesitation, but then the guys started pouring noisily from the train, grabbing everyone's attention, and he relaxed.

He searched for something to say about her new glasses. He asked if Nath was around.

She's coming, Marlene answered. She's parking the car. But I'm dead on my feet. It was nonstop today, we just closed up.

A town official had grabbed a mic and was already spewing the usual blah-blah while the guys dropped their duffel bags like turds to sweep up their wife or mother or lift terrified children at arm's length, and others headed rowdily to the watering hole where they were serving beer and refreshments.

Luckily, they didn't celebrate the heroes' return every day. Dan's legs began to shake, seeing all those boys who would soon tip into suffering and never come out.

Well, that's some face you're making, Marlene whispered to him. Looks like something's wrong.

Nice glasses, he answered. The wood frames are a nice touch.

Nath joined them a little later, the requisite smile on her lips, making her way through the baby carriages, pregnant women, fused couples, the manics, the zombies. She and Dan exchanged blasé looks. It was a small town. As they knew, it was either this or go to Mass on Sunday.

Marlene, on the other hand, seemed delighted with the ambiance. She smiled at the mothers, spoke to the children. She took advantage to introduce herself, I'm Nath's sister, I'm moving here, I work with her, it's a beautiful day, I'm so happy to be here, to share this moment with you, I hope we'll see each other again, get to know each other better. To the point where Nath finally grabbed her by the sleeve and dragged her outside, having no desire to spend the night there. She was hungry. So was Dan.

## FOWL

Unlike other girls her age, Mona didn't have a boyfriend and had never had sex. It wasn't what everyone else believed, not even the two or three girls who imagined they knew her well, despite the vagueness she deliberately maintained on the subject. Especially since she was hardly the type to lower her gaze or blush at a sexual allusion. She had managed to forge a reputation as an experienced young woman without ever having to go through it, but she was the only one who could admire her handiwork. Even her own mother—and God knew that Nath had investigated the matter—couldn't say for sure.

She was in no hurry; she got along just fine on her own. She didn't see what was so urgent about throwing yourself into the arms of the first doofus to come along. If it was just to be like everyone else, or like her mother, thanks anyway. She had something else in mind.

It had been dark for a while, and she was going a bit stir-crazy when Dan came to pick her up.

You took your time, she said.

He shrugged one shoulder. The living room wasn't a mess. He appreciated it, without letting it show. The train was late getting in, he said.

First of all, I'm not hungry. And I'm also having my period.

And the connection is . . .

I'm not in the mood, that's the connection. I'm not looking forward to seeing her.

He leaned over the kitchen sink to wash his hands. Forced himself to remain calm, expressionless, before the painful spectacle of his tranquility vanishing in a blink if she refused to make peace with her mother and prolonged her stay at his place, sowing a disorder that she thought was invisible—whereas he could follow her every trace, with her scents, her reflections, her hair that he rinsed down with the spray nozzle and that clogged the drain, that he had to dig out with his fingers, her unmistakable presence.

Anyway, your father will be out soon. This won't make him happy. Be smart about it. The first thing we learned was how to stay low. Let things fly over your head, that's my advice.

He wiped his hands vigorously. For an instant, he wondered what she was going to do with her tampons, if he should furnish his bathrooms with little plastic bags before it became a problem—such as waking up one morning with a blocked toilet and Mona shrugging nonchalantly.

The place was packed. The room bathed in an odor of food, alcohol, and sweat—the nights were still chilly, but most of the guys were in T-shirts, like most of the women, one group to show off their biceps, the other their chests, their tattoos, and all this unwrapping required a certain comfort, a certain temperature, they could feel the cold biting every time the door opened onto new arrivals—and the music wasn't great, either, the thousand things you heard a thousand times, but Nath and Marlene had taken off their coats and were waving their bare arms at them.

After they were seated, and mother and daughter had exchanged a few furtive glances, Nath grabbed up the menu and proclaimed that they shouldn't get fish, the season was over.

Marlene ordered a martini. Nath looked daggers at her. Marlene chose to ignore it and appeared delighted to see her niece, laid a grateful hand on hers. We waited for you to order, she said. We just had drinks.

Nath folded the menu and looked at her daughter. I took the opportunity to change your sheets, she said. I'm sure you understand.

Dan got up to fetch the drinks. He hoped the hardest part would be over by the time he returned to his seat, and the mere thought of returning home and finding the place empty left him almost euphoric.

It was time for Richard to take back the reins. Dan observed the three women at the table across the room and instinct told him to keep his distance, not butt in. Richard was in for no fun. Managing those three, holding out on all fronts—forget it, the task seemed insurmountable. He wouldn't have wanted to trade places. He wished him luck.

Whatever the case, Mona's bag was packed. Dan himself had put it on the back seat while she remained silent, with a faraway look. He reckoned that bag made her departure inevitable, that there was no turning back.

I've given her back her room, Marlene announced.

He hadn't seen that one coming. On the spur of the moment, he found nothing to say.

I'll manage, she finally added, looking away.

He didn't take the bait. She could think what she liked. The fact was, she wasn't surprised. She hadn't been here long, but she was starting to get to know him, see which of his screws were a bit loose. A guy with problems.

Nath had explained all that to her, that nearly all of them came back with a marble missing, something broken. A few of them were at the bar, planted there since they'd leaped off the train, staring at a Beyoncé video with vacant eyes, as if they were knocked out standing. And yet they were strong guys, perfectly healthy-looking.

Will you buy me a drink, she asked.

Listen, he answered, don't ask me to put you up. I hope you won't take that the wrong way.

No, that's kind of you, but I have a room at the hotel. Until I can find a place.

He nodded, looked at her a moment, longer than he would have liked, without making any headway in deciding whether the woman was fish or fowl. Her wood-framed glasses didn't help. He glanced around him. It was a small town.

## COMMUNITY

Drop your guard, even for a second, and you could wind up stone dead or caught in some implausible situation that would turn your life upside down, make you into some other person you never would have become had you remained vigilant. Dan knew what he was talking about. He was able to go for days straight without shutting his eyes. The other guys slept soundly when it was his watch.

He grimaced at her.

Does it bother you if people see us together, she asked.

No, it doesn't bother me.

That's how it seems to me, Dan. I might be wrong, but I get the impression you're tense.

Why would I be tense. I'm happy to see things return to normal. It's probably just exhaustion. I adore Mona, but I'm glad she's going home. Inviting herself to my place didn't help anybody.

Marlene nodded. It was becoming complicated with him; things didn't progress much. She had quickly understood that Dan was more or less part of the family and that she'd do well to stay on his good side, but he didn't hold up his end. At least he wasn't hostile. Which at this point, with a little distance, she considered a minor miracle.

She glanced over at their table.

Looks like it's going okay, she said. I don't think they'll exactly kiss and make up, but still.

Let's bring them their drinks, he said.

Outside the sky was clear, a deep black. They hugged goodbye on the sidewalk while Nath fished for her house keys. It was midnight. Eucalyptus trees were getting shredded in the keen air, waving their torn leaves in front of her house.

Nath said she'd make something simple for Richard's return, maybe lasagna, there wasn't much to celebrate. Dan moved to pick up Mona's bag but the girl beat him to it. He could expect her not to say a word to him for weeks to come; it was the price he had to pay. He raised his collar and watched the three women filing into the house. He shut his eyes a moment before tearing himself away.

In front of his house, he ran into his neighbor, a guy who lived with his wife and kids and went off to work every morning in a suit, behind the wheel of his hybrid. A dentist or something; the family went to church on Sundays. He had thrown a duffle coat over his pajamas and was dragging a briard on a leash in the moonlight.

This neighborhood reminds me of Switzerland, he announced. The calm, the quiet, the clean streets. You feel safe here, especially when you've got kids. We try to raise them the best we can, right. Adults have to set an example.

You didn't have to think too hard to read between the lines. A retiree lived across the street, a former accountant whose wife had up and left him without a word. Farther on, the house of a judge, the one who had given Richard three months without parole. In another, with its flowered white balcony, an angry-looking woman raised her Down syndrome child who spent his time in the pool, shouting and making faces. A community. It had taken them time to accept him, bury their distrust—the guys coming home from those distant massacres were always troublemakers, misfits, hotheads—to finally admit that by some miracle they had inherited the only more or less palatable veteran, with his regular job, his willingness to lend a hand, and polite into the bargain. Rather than some alcoholic, violent, raving, hairy junkie.

Unlike Richard, Dan felt it was best to toe the line, keep a low profile while trying to get back on his feet, resume a normal life, and he wouldn't get there by hanging out with the local zombies, drawing attention to himself. It was hard enough as it was.

In that regard, Mona clearing out was for the best. You never knew. The crystal ball could blow apart at any moment, at the slightest infraction. At any moment they could rise up and expel him, one way or another. Richard laughed at him when they talked about it. He had an excellent reason: he hated people. They didn't exist for him. Except when they threw him behind bars.

You don't agree, the dentist insisted in an affable tone. Dan nodded with a knowing smile. Then he lowered his head and locked the car, activating the alarm system, while the briard calmly peed against a tree under his master's self-satisfied gaze.

Once inside, before even turning on the lights, he headed straight to the bathroom to wash his hands. The water still came out of the faucet ice cold in late March. After a moment, it was scalding. No matter, what a relief to be there, finally alone again. Take a few sleeping pills and go to bed. Strain his ears and not detect a living soul. Not the slightest presence. He pressed the pedal of the garbage can and threw out a perfumed soap that Mona had left behind. He stood for a moment with his hands under the water, observing the furious flow in his sink. Tough day. Nonetheless, he launched into a bout of ironing. In the twilight—he was used to it—and in front of the wide-open window, despite the stinging cold, he felt like himself. He always delayed the moment when he would shut his eyes and turn toward the wall, pulling the sheet over him.

# AUSPICIOUS

A few days before his release, Richard took advantage
of the first wafts of spring, of a blue sky whose color
alone changed everything, especially women's moods—
who knew why—to announce to Nath that he had
acquired a new car.

She stiffened a bit as he said it, even though he admitted only a third of the Alfa's price. Her thoughts were
racing at a hundred miles an hour; she weighed the pros
and cons in less than a quarter of a second.

Is this really the right time, she pretended to worry.
And she gave a weak sigh, the kind someone who's too
softhearted might give an unruly child.

Can you see me getting around this city on foot, he said,
pointing a thumb at himself. I can't.

She nodded, with the hint of a pale smile toward the
barred windows so he wouldn't feel he'd won too easily.
I mean, it's pretty expensive, she defended herself
limply. It's kind of an extravagance, don't you think.

He took her hands and leaned in toward her. At that
moment, she noticed that he'd been boiling inside for
the last several minutes, that he was burning up, but
no surprise there, she had taken care to select an outfit
that wouldn't leave him indifferent after three months
of abstinence or God knew what. She made sure not to
neglect any opportunity, to sharpen all her defenses in
anticipation of Richard's return. If she played her cards

right, nothing would explode in their faces, no fires would start. She tugged on her skirt.

For some time, their conjugal life had been nothing to write home about. And now here was her husband, with shining eyes and a dry mouth. In reality, they were driven by an animal, primal instinct that was almost comic. Richard's forehead was beaded with sweat and he was kneading her hands without realizing what he was doing, lower lip brooding, cock stiff inside his cotton pants.

She thought about the guy she sometimes hooked up with, who was already stammering by dessert, salivating for it. It was laughable. Maybe due to the arrival of spring.

I know what you're thinking, but fuck them, Richard declared with clenched teeth. Don't get involved.

I thought I might buy a flat screen TV, she said with a shrug. But no biggie, it'll keep.

Great. I can't wait to come home.

As soon as she turned to leave, he lit a cigarette and gazed after her. He could have done worse. Of all the girls he'd known, Nath was the one best suited to him. He was still convinced of that nearly twenty years later, despite all their highs and lows. The only girl who had weathered his storms, his repeated absences, the only one who had stood up to him—rightly so, in the final account, and clear-sightedly, but the present was all that mattered, and regrets never got you anywhere.

The purchase of the Alfa had gone pretty smoothly, without much haggling, and Richard was still feeling the buzz, colored by a strong sexual appetite for his wife that the circumstances rekindled.

During his recreational walk, he let it be known that he was looking for a flat screen, top of the line, at a good price. And the guy who'd sold him the Alfa happened to have a cousin who could find him one.

Darkness was falling as he lay on his cot, wondering if Nath felt the same impatience he did, if desire was eating away at her, if she too was touching herself at that moment. They had kind of begun neglecting each other as time went by, especially since his return from Iraq, which had knocked him for a bigger loop than he let on. He thought about the time they'd wasted. Then of the pleasure he'd find again as soon as the Alfa was ready. He had ordered magazines on Amazon to familiarize himself with it. No pictures of naked women pinned to *his* wall.

His upcoming release and Mona's return sped things up, and Marlene moved into a furnished studio not far away—a five-minute walk from there. Not exactly cheery, but she only used it for sleeping. Her days were long and tiring: no one would have thought there could be so many dogs in this town, friendly ones, trembling ones, mean ones, and night was already falling by the time they closed up shop and dragged a sack full of fur of all types, lengths, and colors to the garbage bins. Marlene had blisters on her fingers from the shears. And on the trip home, it was late and they didn't have the energy to hold a real conversation about their various troubles. They ate haphazardly, whatever they could find, or else they ordered pizza, or empanadas, or sushi that they gulped down in the kitchen while Mona brought her plate in front of the TV and sat cross-legged—Nath didn't want to confront her or criticize anything until Richard came home and she could relieve herself of some of the burden Mona represented. There was no magic key. No chance that problems would be solved overnight—if ever. But at least she could breathe. She could breathe twice as deeply, as she was ridding herself of Marlene by the same token and that was no small matter. In the evening, when she locked up, she would have given a bundle for her sister to vaporize on the sidewalk and not reappear until morning. We'd all like to have that power, at least once or twice in life.

She tried not to think about Marlene being pregnant. Thinking about it left her feeling utterly demoralized. Now and then she cast sidelong glances at her sister, and it was so strange for her to be there, so improbable after all those years of separation and all those memories floating to the surface, everything she thought she'd forgotten, that she remained speechless, in a state of disbelief. As if she didn't have her own problems to contend with.

In the evening, when she went to bed, she sat upright for a moment, chin resting on her knees, and stared at the empty shape next to her, Richard's spot, and after that she had trouble sleeping despite her fatigue, and she felt that before long she wouldn't be able to stand the sight of another dog. Or another soldier. Or a single member of her family. She had been telling herself this for years. Since Mona was very small. Then came the moment when she took a sleeping pill, or even two, and fell asleep, often with fists clenched.

She had long ago realized that Richard was incorrigible, but also that he was the solid one—even if these days he seemed less reliable.

She decided not to get up late the next morning and grimaced when she saw the weather, gray sky, windy. No doubt these were the last dark, chilly days before the arrival of spring. Richard wouldn't be out for several hours, but that left little time to hope for the sky to clear, and she'd no doubt need an umbrella—praying that they'd be spared a hailstorm.

Marlene had decided to bake a pie but she started to whine because of the blisters on her hands. So much so that Dan finally turned from the window and asked half-heartedly if he could help.

In less than a second, she had tied an apron around his waist. His Special Forces reflexes were no longer what they had been. Mona and her mother glanced at each other in amazement.

The evening before, at the bowling alley, Marlene had again blacked out, and if Dan hadn't been there to catch her she would have keeled over and collapsed to the floor like a limp rag. That's the second time I've come to in your arms, she'd said with a laugh, ignoring Dan's embarrassed look as he cast about for a corner to dump her in. He stretched her out on the first bench he saw, in a clatter of bowling pins.

Nath began to wonder, curious, concerned, whether her sister wasn't trying to pick Dan up, whether such a thing was possible, whether she'd soon have to pinch herself. She looked at Dan for a moment with his apron and his rolling pin. The sky was beginning to clear when she shoved in the baking dish of lasagna she had made, the wind was chasing away the clouds, the sun hadn't yet pierced through but was getting close.

Setting foot outside, Richard squinted. Then he took out his sunglasses. Dan was waiting a bit farther on. They smiled, gave each other a high five, a brief hug, then Richard got into the passenger seat and they headed off. The women were waiting with a smile. Nath had invited a young couple to liven things up a bit, keep it from seeming too much like a family reunion and more like a Sunday meal among friends, and they had already had several glasses of punch by the time the couple showed up. Ralph got around in a wheelchair and Gisele was a nurse. She'd assisted with his double amputation and that's when it had clicked between them, according to her.

Ralph turned toward Marlene and said it was a souvenir he'd brought back from the Middle East, of a fierce

battle, door to door, house to house, and anyway he'd
be dead if Richard and Dan hadn't pulled him out of
there, dragged him into a building riddled with bullet
holes in the mind-blowing heat. Those two were really
two of a kind, he added, nodding heavily. It's thanks to
them I'm here to tell you all this, Marlene. Fire on all
sides. From everywhere. Enough to drive you insane.
She almost touched his hand but made do with a smile.
Remarkably, the sky was now empty of the slightest
cloud—this was the kind of thing that told you Richard
had a lucky star. A bright sun passed by in force, like a
fanfare announcing his release from prison.
We've got time, he said.
Dan glanced at him to make sure he'd heard right, but
Richard looked completely serious.
They're waiting for us, Dan pointed out.
No sweat. We won't be long.
Dan gave a vague shrug and turned the car in a different
direction. Arguing would have been pointless. And he
didn't have to choose sides. It was their issue, not his.
They took a detour. The owner of the Alfa was barely
awake when they arrived. He hobbled down the stairs
toward them in boxer shorts, with a forced smile. Hey,
Richard, he exclaimed, looks like you're back.
Richard signaled for him to open his garage.
They took their time. They examined the Alfa from
every angle. Richard ran his fingers over the body without hiding his pleasure while the other hovered around

him, the Alfa this, the Alfa that, but Richard wasn't listening. He just exchanged a few misty-eyed glances with Dan and continued his inspection.

Meanwhile, the others had ended up sitting down to dinner and drinking more wine, telling each other about themselves and dragging things out. The lasagna got cold on the table. Nath's features had darkened. They were now an hour late and not answering their phones. She felt her blood beginning to boil. Richard's homecoming was not getting off to an auspicious start. Ralph squeezed her shoulder. They'll be here, he said. I wouldn't get worked up about it.

She nodded. She said that everyone should serve themselves. Ralph pushed back in his wheelchair to grab some beers from the fridge and Gisele lit a cigarette. Despite everything, the sun was shining outside, the trees budding.

Dan kept to the sidelines while Richard and Alfa Man haggled over the price. The sky was now a bright blue. We're gonna have our heads handed to us, Richard admitted once they were on their way.

Dan nodded. She's going to be livid, he said, eyes fixed on the road.

# BEESWAX

During the three months he'd spent in prison, Richard had acquired the bad habit of getting up early, at the crack of dawn. No comparison with Dan, of course, who was up at four in the morning and started his exercise routine well before daybreak, in the chill of pitch-black night, summer and winter—but if that was the only way he could avoid going crazy, it was his business.

Richard loathed discipline. Especially when it involved an alarm clock. He even hated the colors of daybreak, its insipid hues, its second-rate silence, and all the sorry poetizing it inspired; while dusk, the reddish glow of sunset, the day's surrender, had a whole other aspect. Slipping into the night while your brain emptied itself with no intention of reviving, *that* took guts, he mused while drinking his coffee. The house was quiet, the women asleep. Especially Nath, who had given her all until two in the morning, with the devil's own desire, a resolution that surprised him, that had taken him back years, to when their bouts were truly epic. She had rolled onto her side with a groan, saying she was dead in a barely audible voice.

Watching the dew that formed an aureole at the bottom of the window panes and trembled in the dawn light filtering through the leaves of a flowering camellia, he thought about Marlene, that strange creature who had stood before him, who had finally taken off her glasses and thrown her arms around his neck in accordance with the laws governing relations between brother-in-law and sister-in-law, and who had seemed even spacier to him than at their last, long-ago meeting, in another city, at another time—or anyway, no better.

In this house, he was the last to bed and the last one up, and things were not about to change. He didn't like feeling alone, the silence hurt his ears and if it lasted too long, he had to stop himself from screaming—and there were others who were worse off, others who couldn't hear a thing or had skulls crushed to a pulp, who sobbed like infants at the drop of a hat; he shouldn't complain, just take some pills and roll with it. Ralph was a good example. He stood up to it even without his legs. Not very bright, but solid. Force of will.

Richard remembered dragging him to shelter, the remnants of his legs lost under the rubble, while an explosion disemboweled a wall behind them. In complete silence, while a cloud of dust enveloped them, a shower of debris rained down on their heads. And Ralph who seemed to be yelling at the top of his lungs, mouth twisted beyond recognition, eyes full of tears, but Richard didn't hear a thing, the sound was off. He had never lived through anything so terrifying, as if he'd been ejected out of the world, and still today it was his worst nightmare.

It was just seven in the morning. For a moment, he thought of going back to bed. The sooner he got into a good rhythm, the sooner he'd fucking well forget about his stretch of time in the shadows—where he had gained twelve pounds, all bad fat.

He raised his eyes toward Nath, who was crossing the kitchen in her skimpies. She stationed herself in front of the window and asked with a yawn if he'd fallen out of bed.

He sniggered.

The backyard was barely emerging from the twilight in which a few thin patches of icy snow still shone, crystalline, while the horizon brightened in a sudden halo above the surrounding woods. Nath sighed. Her approaching forties were starting to make themselves felt. She moved aside to get out of the frame, eliminate her reflection in the glass.

Richard gazed at her a moment, then glanced at his watch and decided they didn't have time. Drop me off on the way, he said to her. As she passed by within reach, he nonetheless extended a friendly hand toward his wife's behind, which she adroitly dodged.

His arm was still reaching into the void when Marlene knocked on the windowpane. She was wearing a striped wool cap pulled down over her ears, and a slight white mist drifted from her mouth. He signaled for her to go around the house and went to open the door.

In the bedroom, Nath called that she'd be out in five minutes.

Take your time, Marlene called back, smiling at Richard, and she added for him alone, with an exaggerated wink, I'm not the one in charge here.

They'd had a fair amount to drink the night before, and Richard had come to Marlene's defense when Nath had criticized her sister's alcohol consumption. The episode had elicited some tension on both sides, especially since Nath wasn't in the habit of being a killjoy for no reason—in the end she had simply given up, kept quiet about the pregnancy, and had given Marlene a jet-black look while raising a toast to her health.

The memory of the evening, of the conversation that had ended on the thought that people were old enough to know what was best and should mind their own beeswax, relaxed Richard. By and large, Marlene was proving less annoying than he'd feared, and if she didn't come around too often, if she kept the necessary distance, he might be able to put up with her. And Nath would be grateful to him.

Coming back into the kitchen, he asked if she still conked out like that.

She vaguely shrugged. It happens now and then, she answered.

He looked at her for a moment without saying anything, as if pondering what she'd just told him.

Then Nath entered and they got into her car that smelled of wet dog. It was now completely light, sparrows were flitting about the sky, gathering in clusters on the power lines and bobbing together in the cool air. The radio announced fifty-seven degrees, slight wind, clear skies.

Nath stopped at the supermarket to get gas. Richard turned around to Marlene, whose eyes had been fixed on the back of his close-shaven neck. You used to be married, didn't you, he said.

She drifted for a moment. Yes, once upon a time, she answered, and as Richard pensively shook his head, she added that it wasn't worth talking about.

I see, he replied. It's hard to find the right person.

He added to himself that you only needed to look around you, the old, the ugly, the wraiths leaning on shopping carts, the guys who hung around parking lots with a beer, a sandwich, and baleful eyes.

I think I wasn't the right person, she sighed.

That could be too, he said.

## HEART

Dan had spent a very bad night and had to dig deep into his reserves to finish his jog, cutting short his squats to take a double dose of aspirin. Ending the evening on Black Russians was never a good idea, but even though his skull was about to explode, he didn't regret it. Nath had greeted them with stony silence—not so terrible, given the alternatives—and everything could still have gone south, there had been a pause, everyone's eyes riveted on her.

He was wondering whether he should leave when Nath walked up to them and kissed Richard full on the mouth.

More than once, she had unnerved him; he had looked at her wide-eyed, with a hint of admiration for the feat she'd just pulled off, and when he talked to Richard about it, when he tried to make him share his awe at such marvels, Richard brushed it aside with a sweep of his hand, claiming all women had that ability in their blood. It's called duplicity, he remarked before changing the subject.

Dan was no expert. He didn't devote much time to girls and wasn't interested enough to form his own opinions about the possible duplicity of women. But that didn't keep him from appreciating the artistry, remaining transfixed like a kid in front of a magic trick.

Whatever the case, they had had a good time, knocked back the booze until nightfall, then gone out to buy the makings of Black Russians, and after that was a black hole. A cold shower partly dispelled his headache and he joined Richard, who was counting his cash in the middle of the street, in front of the bank. The weather was warm. Nath had dropped him off a few minutes ear-lier and they decided to get coffee before going to take delivery of the Alfa.

Guys spun about on their stools when Richard walked in and he greeted some of them, exchanging a few words while Dan grabbed a menu and ordered a tomato juice and fried eggs. There was a time, back in the good old days, when he used to gobble them raw. He hadn't known how to stop in time. And now things were hard. Sometimes atrociously hard. Especially since he couldn't see the end of the tunnel. Richard had paused at the counter to settle a few outstanding bills and signaled that he'd have the same.

Dan checked a phone message relaying that the motor of a pinsetter had burned out and the lane was shut down until further notice. If I were you, I'd call back quick, the caller's voice had added. He knew. No point thinking twice about it.

I'll just go and come right back, he said, standing up. Richard, I'll be back in half an hour, take your time finishing up.

Richard frowned, hesitated, concentrated on the fried eggs shimmering in his plate, annoyed by this hitch in plans. Since when have you been an electrician, he went, not raising his eyes.

Heading out of town, traffic was held up by a cattle hauler overturned in a ditch. A few calves and sheep were still struggling out, in shock, stumbling along the roadside, trying to find their way amid the bright shrubs and scattered undergrowth, bleating and lowing ceaselessly.

He looked at his watch—a Lip he'd gotten as a free gift, along with a tablet, for subscribing to the Book of the Month Club—and sighed.

First of all, there was no way he was sticking his hands in an electric motor. But the owner of the alley couldn't care less about legalities, especially when it came to her employees, cleaning women, handymen, maintenance guys, and so on.

I didn't catch that, she answered, cupping her ear.

Listen, I don't know how these gizmos work.

Didn't they teach you anything in the army, besides how to kill people. He stared at her for a moment, speechless. You could hear the clack of bowling balls, their faraway drumrolls, pins flying in all directions with a sound of bamboo or castanets. If you weren't used to it, the concert soon became unbearable, and Brigitte, the manager, didn't spend much time there. He could see she was starting to get uncomfortable, with her grimaces and sighs, and he felt like prolonging the pleasure of watching her twist in the wind.

But he was anxious about keeping his job. It formed part of his will to regain control, and he wasn't going to squander all that work, all the time spent rebuilding a normal life, getting back in line; he wasn't about to let all that go just for a small, fleeting enjoyment. Fine, since I'm here, he said, looking up at the apparently kaput motor that stank of burnt rubber. I'll see what I can do. I'll do my best.

The old hag relaxed. It's important we understand each other, she said, if you're going to work for me.

The minute she turned her back, he called Richard, who must have been wondering where the hell he was.

Don't give me your excuses, the latter cut him off in a flat voice. You let me down, fuckface.

He tried calling back but the phone rang unanswered. He swore under his breath.

Night was falling when Dan finished putting away his tools, looking preoccupied. Yes, he'd had some trouble with that goddam motor, but he was able to dismantle and reassemble an assault rifle in fifty-two seconds flat, defuse a landmine with a blindfold on; it's not as if he were one-handed. A few minutes earlier, he'd put the lane back in service and Brigitte, behind the glass screen of her office, had congratulated him with a brief thumbs-up.

He settled at the bar in front of a pale ale that he rotated between his fingers, staring at it fixedly. Now and then, a car left the road to enter the parking lot, and its head-lights danced on the false laminate ceiling.

He was about to check whether he'd heard from Richard when Marlene suddenly hoisted herself onto the next stool. Good thing you're here, she said, leaning toward him. I can't seem to get rid of this guy.

He turned to the individual in question, who was hovering a few feet away, and threw him a brief glance before turning back to Marlene.

I hope I'm not disturbing you, she said.

He shook his head.

Normally he wasn't very talkative, but this business with Richard weighed heavy on his heart, and since Marlene said he looked worried and seemed ready to listen, he let himself go without giving it much thought and spoke his piece, leaving nothing out. After which, he felt better. It was almost disconcerting.

She didn't see what he had to blame himself for. Richard should have been more understanding, less impulsive. She touched his arm.

He picked up their beers and they went out for a smoke. It wasn't too cold, the air smelled good, the night was calm, and no one was expecting them. A crescent of moon rose over the distant cliffs bathed in darkness below the horizon line.

It's rare for it to be so warm after dark this time of year, he said. It's funny. We're going to have an early spring. Oh, I see what you mean. It's so sad, really. Entire continents will disappear.

It's going to happen faster than we think. They've just announced that they got their forecasts messed up. It's possible you and I will experience it. We'll be old but we'll still be here to see it. To cheer it on.

It makes you feel like strolling along the road, walking in the darkness, she said vaguely.

He nodded and finished his beer while looking up at the sky. For her part, she found it very strange that he didn't have a girlfriend.

# VOICE

Richard finally gave a sign of life just as Dan was dropping Marlene off in front of her house. He hadn't chosen the best moment to resurface, for Dan's mind was elsewhere; he hadn't totally forgotten him, but close enough. He hadn't felt the time pass with Marlene. And so he was almost taken aback when he saw Richard's name displayed on the screen, almost annoyed. He gave Marlene a wave and answered the phone without pleasure, especially since he'd felt good that evening, talking quietly, finally relaxed, and even before Richard opened his mouth he already knew it was fucked. Richard was going to ruin everything.

You gotta come get me, he said in a strangled voice punctuated by a moan, and God knew Richard was no softie.

Dan felt as if he'd been doused by an icy shower. Then a wave of guilt washed over him and he set off immediately, brow furrowed, mood dark.

Meanwhile, Richard managed to drag himself to a bench at the edge of the reservoir whose surface gleamed in the heavy silence. The area was deserted, not a soul around. His thoughts were full of static, muddled by the jolts running through his body. He could hardly explain how he'd ended up there, half dazed, in the dark, but he knew he'd taken a good beating. He checked vaguely that he still had all his teeth, noted that his nose was

bleeding—he tilted his head back and a flock of ducks,
flying out from the reeds, crossed his field of vision—
but apparently nothing was broken, or maybe just a rib
or two. A real miracle. He wouldn't say no to a bit of
morphine, if offered.

He was covered in blood from his nose. He stood up
with difficulty, gritting his teeth, and knelt by the water's edge to rinse his face. The backs of his hands were
swollen—he remembered covering his balls when he
was on the ground, and a good thing, too. He wiggled
his fingers for a moment in the cold water, then let himself drop onto his side, in an inch or two of fresh water.
He was a wreck and all his money was gone.

Dan had Advil in his glove compartment. And so Richard stopped wincing, stood up straight, leaning slightly
against the fridge—his right knee hurt—and claimed
that everything was fine, that it was nothing, that they'd
examined him, a couple of bandages and a bag of frozen
peas would do the trick, while Nath remained planted in
front of him, eyes shining, arms wrapped tight around
her as if she'd been seized by a fierce chill.

I've had worse, he argued. Just imagine if you were a
boxer's wife.

She shrugged in ill humor and went back to bed.

It had been a long time since she'd tried to fathom the
how and why of Richard's activities—his plans, his
shady deals, his schemes—for not only did he refuse
to talk about them, but he had no intention of making

the situation better, of changing the slightest thing, and when she had understood this, when she'd become aware of the walls he'd built around himself, she realized that he had ripped out half her heart.

Yemen. Iraq. Afghanistan. The man the army had sent back to her was not the same one she'd first met. Everyone here knew how these things ended up, but no one wanted to believe it until a son or husband or father returned from there with a screw loose and raised hell and spent the day lying about on the living room sofa watching TV and snarfing potato chips or lord knew what else. And then, they understood. The wicked sleight of hand. The women realized the trick that had been played on them. Nath had cried for an entire day when her heart had broken.

Yemen. Iraq. Afghanistan. Places you'd like to visit on holiday. Except that she and Mona had not taken a single holiday since Richard had left the army. With his frickin' PTSD, his microscopic pension, and all the crap he had to take.

And that was the man who was going to come lie down beside her. With all his weight, all his superiority, all his ignorance. The man who was going to stick his finger in her, rub his dick against her ass. While she knew less and less about him, gave only the most cursory glance at his comings and goings—as if keeping an eye on an irascible, taciturn neighbor.

She heard him talking with Dan and Mona in the
kitchen. If there was still one thing she loved about
him, it was his voice—his voice was what was good in
him, what remained of the love she'd once felt for that
man. She lay with eyes open in the dark, barely breathing. She pulled the covers over her shoulders, as they'd
shut off the heat at sunrise to save money. The bed was
downright cold. She heard Dan leaving—in his own
way, he was no better.

Mona walked him to the door while Richard lowered his
pants with a grimace and covered his knee with the bag
of frozen peas.

She caught Dan by his sleeve before he could step into
the darkness.

Did you see that, do you see what it's like, she asked.
Was it really such a hassle to have me living with you.
For a second he remained at a loss. You didn't live with
me, he finally answered. Where did you get that idea.
I won't take this much longer, she went on. I have no
intention of sticking around this madhouse.

He walked down the porch's few steps and turned
around. Mona, for fuck's sake, he shouted. Ask me
whatever you want, but not that.

Not what. What are you talking about.

He shook his head in desperation and headed to his car,
zipping up his jacket almost to the eyeballs.

Dan knew a bit more than the others about Richard's occupations, but he tried to stay on the sidelines, join in as little as possible. It wasn't so easy with Richard, who couldn't always control his bitterness when Dan weaseled out, but they'd known each other for so long and had been through so much together that Richard let him be—congratulating him on his preference for the straight and narrow with an evil smile.

They had talked about it a lot after their homecoming, during their two months of convalescence, and let's just say they hadn't managed to agree on the best way to return to civilian life. Nowadays they agreed to disagree. But the fact that on one harrowing, terror-stricken night they'd sworn to look out for one another, sworn that whoever survived would bury the other with his own hands and plant flowers on his grave—that still remained.

It was no joke. It was an unshakable resolution, on which they could rely with no hesitation; an absolute confidence that bolstered them, even in the midst of crisis, the depths of despair.

Dan moved closer to the flames that were rising again now that the lamb had been roasted and taken off the spit. The local news had mentioned the loss of a half-dozen dazed beasts that had crossed the road and wandered into the dark. The guys had cornered the animal not far from the overturned cattle hauler and slaugh-tered it against the electrified fence of the military base. It had taken three of them. The sheep had been stored overnight in one of their garages, just long enough for them to spread the word, send out invitations, and the others had brought beer and cut up the meat. Cars were parked around the area, not far from the road that ran like a fault through countryside as bald as the moon. With bright enough lights you could get up some speed, be a bit of a cowboy. They listened to old Guns N' Roses on a crappy sound system, but they listened hard and bopped their heads, jumped up and down in place and wailed along with Axl Rose around the crackling campfire.

Soldiers on leave for the most part, new recruits just back from combat zones; you could feel how tense they still were, trying anything to empty their brains as fast as possible.

Marlene was thrilled: she loved lamb. Her cheeks were red and she wasn't the only one with a rosy complexion, as the temperature had dropped quickly after sunset. Incandescent sparks swarmed in the cold air when one of the guys gave a log a solid kick.

I'd like to know where they buy their meat, she said.

He stared at her for a few seconds—flames danced on the lenses of her glasses. Marlene, he said, they didn't buy it. She opened her mouth, then thought better of it and said nothing.

His gaze met Nath's, not far away, who was staring at them with her mind seemingly elsewhere. Which seemed to be her normal state for the past two or three days, in other words since Richard had come home all bashed up. Still, it wasn't the first time something like this happened—one look at their medicine chest told the tale, with most of the shelves taken up by bandages and painkillers. Richard was never the last one to throw a punch and Nath didn't make a fuss, just reminded him about the first aid kit and the bottle of cheap whiskey that she set on the table without a word, wearily, and the next morning she'd already forgotten about it.

But this time was different. Dan knew her well enough. Something was eating at her. And no doubt a whole load of somethings, if you put yourself in her shoes, if you added up all the irritations she had to face these days. Richard had insisted she go with them or she wouldn't have come; this meant nothing to her.

But Richard had been chatting with some pals for a while now and she was clearly getting fed up.

Dan walked by her on his way to a beer.

Listen, she said to him. There's something I have to tell you. Now that we're alone for a second.

He looked at her and vaguely nodded. She appeared so bothered, so conflicted over what she wanted to say, without managing to get it out, that it seemed like a pressing need.

Go on, I'm listening, he encouraged, leaning into the cooler.

She was standing behind him, her lips pinched, ready to spill it all. Looking up, she noticed Marlene who had remained standing near the campfire, lit up like a Madonna, a blanket around her shoulders, and all of Nath's drive vaporized in an instant. She lowered her head. Off to one side, a bunch of guys were revving their motorcycles. Dogs barked on the road.

So what is it, he said, pulling open the tab.

Oh, I don't know, she answered with a sigh of exhaustion. I hope I'm wrong.

She sometimes had the impression that Dan understood her implicitly, that in this regard he was more perceptive than Richard, but here he evidently wasn't following her at all. He looked like a deer in headlights.

She stared hard at him a moment, then declared that she'd had enough and wanted to go home. He didn't try to hold her back. That, at least, he knew would be wasted effort. He preferred to save his energy for the almost inevitable day when Richard discovered that she had, so to speak, run a bit wild during his absence. He went off into the shadows to piss quietly while watching Nath head to her car, and thought to himself she was going through a tough time, lots of upsets, and there was nothing he could do about it. He buttoned his fly. The music was still loud but he had left the first decibel-saturated circle, the shadows enveloped him, and his relative distance from the crowd and empty bladder offered him a little respite beneath the starry sky.

I was looking for you, my blanket caught fire, Marlene announced. I think I'm a jinx.

Dan lowered his gaze onto the blanket in question and, indeed, half the fringes were charred.

It could have been worse, she continued. I felt myself drifting away. But I'm okay. Sorry about your blanket. This kind of thing only happens to me.

It happens all the time. I can't tell you how many drunk guys I've seen stumble into the embers. Or how many I've seen set themselves on fire with just a candle.

She looked at him for a moment and shivered. What's the matter with her, she asked.

He shrugged. Mmm, she claims she doesn't know. She's worried about being wrong. I'm just repeating what she told me.

If she fell down, Marlene said pensively, she would never tell us where it hurt. Her eyes would tear up, but she just gritted her teeth, that's all. She hasn't changed. She turns on the radio while we're working so we don't have to talk, can you imagine. Mom used to pull her hair out with her. It's like I'm by myself—I spend my days with cats and dogs.

I almost got a dog, you know, he segued, a basenji, but when I heard it howl, I brought it right back. I told the guy he could keep the deposit. I certainly intend to, he said, but anyway, I get your point.

Across the street, some guys were playing at rodeo, dust flew about, and an odor of oil and burnt rubber slowly settled over everything. It was good to see them having fun, finally decompressing after aging ten years in a few weeks, and the girls cutting loose, thrilled to be with their boyfriends again. Enjoy it while you can, he said to himself.

I like your sense of humor, she said. Sometimes I don't understand it right away.

Come off it, I don't have any sense of humor. I lost all that. It's like smiling, I still have trouble with it.

But it's coming along, right.

These things always take a long time. It's a lot to digest. I'm glad spring's almost here, I'll be able to putter in my garden. I can't wait to trim my hedges.

It was two in the morning by the time he parked in front of her house.

At that moment, he said, I felt like my spirit had left my body and I was terrified. I could tell I wasn't dead, but I wasn't alive either. Not sure how to explain it. I thought I was going nuts. I didn't lose my legs, like Ralph did, and I'm not comparing my suffering with his, but I've had a taste of it, Richard has had a taste of it, everyone here has had a taste of it one way or other. And good luck leaving it behind. Trust me, you're not out of the woods yet. Have fun trying to get your life together. Dan, I've watched you, you know, I've watched you going about living. I think that meeting people, going out, having some fun wouldn't be such a bad thing for you. Teach me how to bowl, for instance. Let's go to the movies, I don't know, or for a walk. I'll give you my arm, since you don't have a girlfriend. I'm practically your sister-in-law. A guy walking alone always looks a bit dodgy.

Okay. We'll see. We can sleep on it.

You don't have to, you know.

If it was a drag, I'd say so. It's not a drag at all. We can always go get a drink.

It would be good for me too. Sometimes I feel like I'm suffocating with Nath. I have to go out and accost someone in the street just to get a bit of conversation.

Listen, I've seen this before. I wouldn't worry about it too much if I were you. It'll get better after a while.

Suddenly he leaned toward the windshield and raised his eyes to the sky. It's going to be nice tomorrow. We could go to the drive-in. They're showing *Lost Highway* in the early evening. I never get tired of seeing it.

It's been ages since I've gone. The man I was living with hated movies. He worked in a bank.

They're all shitheads, those guys who work in banks. My father was a banker. He died in 2007, just at the time of the crash. He's rotting in hell as we speak. I never saw him think for one second about anyone but himself. It never crossed his mind.

She rested a hand on his arm before getting out. Tell me, what do you mean by getting back to a normal life.

He blinked, tilted his head to one side. What do you think. It means just what it sounds like, doesn't it. She contented herself with a smile. His eyes followed her as she crossed the headlights walking around the car. She was still smiling. Before going inside, Marlene turned back to him.

I'll get the tickets, she said.

He remained motionless a few seconds while she disappeared. At that hour, the town was dead, the lively neighborhoods deserted, the curtains drawn, and he drove home without paying attention. He couldn't believe he'd suggested that idiotic idea, and wondered what had come over him. He washed his hands thoroughly when he got back, then took a long shower and sat for a moment on his bed, clock in hand, hesitating to set the alarm.

He was already thinking that they'd have to arrive early to grab a spot near the exit.

He took his pills and lay down. In the end, he didn't set the alarm, hoping to sleep in a little by skipping his exercise routine. Despite the darkness in the room, there was a ray of moonlight filtering above the shades, and the more he stared at it, the brighter it grew. He felt a thudding in his temples. At least he'd get to see *Lost Highway* again, and on a big screen. After all, it was easier than teaching her how to bowl. Less of a commitment. When she had touched his arm, he'd nearly jumped.

Richard finagled a reprieve on paying off the Alfa and
that same day, he had the eighty-inch-wide screen that
they'd talked about installed in the living room.

Money didn't grow on trees. When he called the guy
to talk about the problem and asked if he couldn't see
his way clear to working it out, the man had snorted on
the other end of the line. Then Richard had swallowed
his pride and asked again. And how do you expect to
pay me, the other had snickered. By sucking me off, or
cleaning my pool for the next twenty years. What do
you take me for, an idiot.

Richard couldn't tell Nath that he'd emptied out her
bank account and then had the money stolen from him.
Impossible. Never. There were limits, a line you didn't
cross. Getting yourself ripped off like some rookie
clown, taking out a wad of cash to score some speed.
How could he have been so dim-witted. He had choked
with rage, banged his head against the wall, called himself every name in the book.

You still there, the other asked.

That evening, when Nath came home and found the
new TV hanging in the living room, she couldn't entirely hide a slight smile of satisfaction.

Is it big enough, Richard said behind her.

He had spent the afternoon on a cloud, and finally

seeing his wife smile, after the face she'd been pulling
since his return, was worth its weight in chocolates.
A bit more and he might even have forgotten the
bargain he'd struck. He'd regained confidence in his
lucky star—which had faded in the black sky above his
head—and once again felt in good form.
Now go take a gander in the garage, he said.
When he'd opened his eyes, early that morning, his
first thought had been that he was on the edge of a cliff,
the very edge, with no money, no car, and in deep,
deep shit. And now this. This sudden brightness, this
improbable miracle. How fast the wind could turn. Fill
utter darkness with light.
Mona thinks it's cool, he called out, turning on the TV.
Try not to wrap it around a tree, she answered from the
garage.
She went out early for her yoga class. Richard was dis-
appointed that she didn't sit with him on the couch, in
front of their new set: the euphoria he'd been feeling since
his situation had turned around, the warmth coursing
through his entire body, was leaving him aroused.
Okay, Richard, but it can wait until tomorrow. Or
even tonight, if I don't get home too late. And besides,
Mona's here, just down the hall. She might get up for
some water or something. I won't be able to keep from
thinking about it. And anyway, I pay for those classes. I
didn't sign up for nothing.

She was very fond of her night classes. Her legs and back felt better after the day's tensions. Her mind, too. She parked in front of the health club and went the rest of the way on foot. The air was prickly. She walked fast and her breath steamed. There were still traces of salt on the sidewalks.

She sat opposite him in one of those bars with padded vinyl booths where they would meet. It was no doubt the first time he'd seen her in a tracksuit, hair uncoiffed and no makeup; she had done it on purpose. She thought for a second of Richard, the interest he'd shown in her five minutes earlier, but ultimately that was all men thought about—that wasn't why she was there. The bouquet of flowers lying on the bench hadn't escaped her notice.

But that was just it: it had to stop. The flowers, the phone calls, the texts. They'd slept together only about half a dozen times. His name was Vincent, but she'd never called him by his first name. He was young, they'd never had a real conversation, he didn't count. Listen, she said. It's all because of fracking. The price of oil collapsed. They shut down his platform earlier than expected.

Just like that. Overnight.

Yeah, whatever. In any case, we can't see each other anymore. Don't try to call me, don't send me anything. Let's not make a big deal out of it. Trust me. He was in Special Forces for years. I don't need to draw you a picture. I'm

not into living in fear, and I have no desire to keep looking over my shoulder. I don't want any of that.

So what do you want.

She pulled back from the table, smiling, surprised. She
hadn't expected anything so direct.

That's kind of a personal question, isn't it.

I'm curious.

She looked at him for a moment, then grabbed her bag
and left without a word.

The night was dark, the street deserted. He caught up
with her in front of a tattoo parlor whose sign was blinking red on the sidewalk. He grabbed her arm to make
her stop.

You don't even know what you want, he barked. That's
what the problem is.

Who said there's a problem, she replied. Not with you,
in any case.

Vincent's face brightened. That's what I was waiting for,
he said. It's about time you told me something real.

She played for time, feeling vaguely guilty.

Fair enough. I'm sorry. It's not what you want that matters, it's what you can get. There's your answer. Now let
me go.

She resumed walking.

Cut all ties. Not a chance, he said between clenched teeth.
Without slowing down, she cast a sidelong glance at
him. One thing you should learn, she said, is women
hate guys who cling.

They turned at the corner with the Toyota dealership
and arrived in front of her club.

You can't stop me from seeing you, he insisted. I'll come
with my dog. I'll make an appointment.

You wouldn't.

That, and other things I haven't thought of yet.

She stared at him once more, with an intensity that
nailed him to the spot, then turned on her heels
and disappeared inside. She sat in the locker room
a moment before getting into her outfit. Like it or
not, nothing had been settled. In the lotus position,
a moment later, in a discreet aroma of essential oils
and slightly senile New Wave music, she wondered
whether she'd have to kill him.


## FINGER

Richard unloaded the full story on Dan a few days later.
About the delivery he'd have to make, the small ad-
vance he'd received, the Alfa, etc.

Dan was sitting in the grass, drying in the sun, blinking, arms hugging his bent knees. He shook his head.
He'd been calmly watching the three women below
diving off a boulder, and Richard had just yanked him
back to reality, on the dark side.

Count me out, he finally blurted.

I can drive a car without you, Richard huffed. I'll be fine.

Dan bit into an apple. We always took the time to think it through, he said without looking at Richard. We weighed the risks before taking the plunge. We didn't go in with just anybody, we weren't that stupid. We stayed alive, that's what we gained. We didn't gain anything else. We came home naked and empty-handed, and that's it. I'd rather have a dangerous life than a shitty one, I'll say it once and for all.

Sparrows were fighting over crumbs from their picnic. Dan looked over at the women coming out of the water. Anyway, there's something I have to talk to you about, Richard added as they came up. But no rush. Smile.

Dan didn't really feel like smiling after what he'd just heard. You didn't have to be psychic to guess that Richard had gotten mixed up in a sordid affair, nor omniscient to predict he'd do just as he pleased, that nothing could turn him away from the twisted path he'd decided to follow.

He lay back and closed his eyes. They couldn't reform Richard. Those who had tried had come back with head hung low. Nath was the only one (and even then) who had some influence over him and managed to obtain a few paltry results—like getting him to chew with his mouth closed, trim his nails once in a while, not say fuck at the drop of a hat, change his underwear every day—after eighteen years of marriage.

The hardest thing was trying to protect people from themselves, from their ignorance and their folly. Most didn't want to hear it. There came a moment when action was pointless, when feelings were pointless, and God knew that Richard was one of the rare individuals who really mattered to him.

Still, the sun felt good on his skin, a first real springtime sun that had inspired the girls to improvise this picnic on the edge of a hidden lake in the middle of the woods— at less than fifteen minutes' drive, the five of them crammed into the Alfa, the three women screaming when Richard took a bend in the road at top speed, after which he turned around with a huge grin and asked how ya doing girls, with a special wink for Mona. The water was cold but it was the best water in the world, limpid, sparkling, and oh my friends, that staggering blue sky, the different shades of green in the jumble of trees, the birds soaring in flocks.

Dan opened his eyes when he heard Mona shriek. A wasp had stung her. The afternoon was dragging a bit. Richard was making phone calls off to one side. It was turning chilly. Marlene lit a cigarette and signaled for Mona to come closer. Nath was changing out of her bathing suit. Dan saw this kind of tableau, this biblical scene, in his dreams when they were on a mission, in the hellhole.

On the way back, they stopped for a drink. Marlene immediately started on the margaritas. Night was falling, the signs lit up, and there was traffic, entire families, guys in caps rolling in slo-mo, windows down, women's tattooed arms draped over the car doors, children, dogs with tongues hanging out, pizza delivery boys, sandwich trucks. Dan kept an eye on the time.

Mona had wanted to join them for the film and he and Marlene had readily agreed, but now her foot was swollen like a pumpkin. The reasonable thing wasn't the most fun, and Dan, to console her, said if it's okay with your dad, I'll take you one evening this week, doesn't matter if I know it by heart.

Why did you say that, Richard said with a smile. Why did you say if it's okay with your dad. What's wrong with you. She spent an entire week sleeping at your place.

I know. But you weren't here, and now you are, so I'm asking your permission. I don't see what the problem is. If I were in your shoes, I'd rather the guy ask—for permission, that is.

What guy. The guy is you.

Mona fidgeted on her chair and told them to quit it. Dan was about to see the film for the fourth time, but his pleasure was undiminished and he felt perfectly relaxed. Marlene's presence at his side didn't bother him, had stopped bothering him some time ago, for no other reason than he was starting to get used to her and didn't find her as invasive, not to say as much of a pain in the ass, as he had at first.

No matter that she spilled half her beer on his knees and had trouble climbing over the seats to change in back and wrap herself in her beach towel. That was Marlene and you had to take her as she was. Nath had painted a portrait of her sister so disadvantageous that the most patient man in the world would have kept shy of her. But she wasn't as slow on the uptake as Nath made her sound. It was really overdone, he felt, really reductive. While she climbed back into the front seat by the shortest and not least acrobatic path, he rolled down his window and ordered some more beers and two bags of popcorn from an old man who walked up and down the rows of cars pushing a refrigerator cart and wearing a little paper beanie from which a white lock of hair escaped onto his forehead, which he brushed aside with an absent hand while the other hand gave back change—a virtuoso performance.

His arms laden, Dan turned to Marlene and they looked at each other a moment, motionless, then he quickly started lining up his purchases on the shelf between them. It was now pitch black out, the film hadn't started yet, but a short about the building of the Great Wall of China diffused a flickering, candle-like light in the passenger compartment.

Oh, you know, she said, I stopped eating popcorn a long time ago. I almost choked to death once.

I'm not surprised.

I know what you think of me. I don't hold it against you. I meant it's easy to swallow one of those things the wrong way. Anyway, I don't think anything bad about you.

That's nice of you to say.

He shoved a handful of popcorn in his mouth and looked away.

You're so different, you and Richard.

He nodded. A couple was smooching in the next car.

Personally, she resumed, I don't have any friends. I never have. I must not be right for anybody.

The film was about to begin, but he looked at her again. I drive people away, she continued.

He remained silent, not knowing what to answer. She ended up reaching out an uncertain hand and brushing his cheek. He choked back his surprise, tried to pay attention to the screen while Bill Pullman dragged morosely on his cigarette and the speaker vibrated.

Are you here, Dan, are you here with me, she whispered.

He loosened his grip on the steering wheel and lit a cigarette of his own. It was often the best thing to do. Marlene took the opportunity to draw closer and rested her head on his shoulder. He put his arm around her and continued to smoke serenely, as if they had slid into warm water in the heart of a deep forest. A veil of fog blurred the windows and they sat there without moving, for several intoxicating minutes, breathing shallowly.

It's so unexpected, she said, pressing against him. So sudden.

Dan's love life was nonexistent. His sex life was hardly more than a few dead-end hookups that sufficed for

both parties and regular visits to porno sites. And so
distrust mixed with curiosity in his mind, which was
so overtaxed just then that it turned in slow motion. Of
the film, to which he was no longer paying the slightest
attention, all that now reached him was Badalmenti's
haunting soundtrack which methodically undercut
everything.

By the time he became aware of Marlene edging closer
to increase their surface of bodily contact, she was already stretching a nude leg across him and strewing his
neck with small damp kisses.

He decided to react. No longer worrying what would
happen if they let go, he kissed her full on the mouth
and slid a finger into her pussy.


## HORNETS

As she told it, the last satisfying sexual relations she'd
known went back an eternity. She only kept a distant
memory that she no doubt embellished the farther away
it grew, and Dan listened with a distracted ear as dawn
rose and slowly dispersed the shadows in the room. It
was the first time a woman had spent the night there,
and this resulted in some disorder—scattered clothes,
tangled sheets, used Kleenexes, bedside rug flipped
over—which was rather disturbing.

What are you thinking of, she asked.

Smiling, Marlene was straddling him, in a dominant position, sated. Rid of her awful glasses, hair undone, breasts forward, he discovered her in a new light, frankly desirable. Seeing that he was still a little hard, she thought she might suck him off but he'd reached his limit, he was empty and he amiably declined her offer. He got out of bed, quickly gathered up everything lying around, and hightailed it into the bathroom.

He hadn't expected her to come join him in the shower. He remained nonplussed a second, then moved over to make room for her, forcing himself to smile, and when she helped herself to his shampoo, his liquid soap, his bath mitt, his personal hygiene gel, and he had to let her rinse herself off first, which lasted a good ten minutes, he wondered whether it had been a mistake to bring her here, whether he would regret it once he was past the euphoria of sexual novelty.

He relaxed somewhat when it crossed his mind that at this hour, since his neighbor and the neighbor's entire family never missed Sunday Mass, there was no danger of running into them when he and Marlene went outside.

Still, it was best not to delay, not invite criticism, not give people an image of him as some kind of dissolute maniac. By now he couldn't wait to bring Marlene home and come back to straighten up.

They had gotten almost no rest, but she pointed out, as he drove in silence through the still empty neighborhoods, that he ground his teeth in his sleep.

Could be, he said with a vague shrug.

But it's not really a problem, she hastened to add.

As she was about to get out of the car, seeing that he didn't lean toward her or loosen his grip on the wheel, she again caressed his cheek. It's all good, she said in a gentle voice, flashing him a luminous smile.

Fear, blood, and suffering weren't the only things he'd known, but no matter how much he washed and scrubbed, they never left him, always came back, always ended up coloring the rest; a cloud always passed in front of the sun and the brightness faded, the shadows stretched over him and imprisoned him. He was used to it. In some ways, he thought of himself as already dead. Marlene, or whoever, could do nothing about it. Those who had spent time in hell never left it. Always alone, crippled by debts, half crazy. They laid flowers on graves, stuffed themselves full of meds, collected their pensions, terrorized their wives and children. He stopped on the way home to buy a few things. Generic bread, Pop-Tarts, hamburger, sale items, household products. Parking in front of his house, he let the engine idle and closed his eyes for a moment before shutting it off. He took a deep breath. In an atmospheric blend of cum, beer, stale tobacco, and a soupçon of vanilla from Marlene's underarm deodorant.

He set down the shopping bag in the kitchen and returned to his car with a rag and some window cleaner, as well as a pack of wipes to rub down the seats. The

sky was blue, the street bathed in a suffocating calm. He
went at it with the ardor of a man possessed, aired out
the vehicle, emptied the ashtray into the gutter, gathered
up one by one the pieces of popcorn that had escaped
in the heat of the action, slid the seats forward to shake
out the floor mats, and froze an instant when he discovered Marlene's small pale-pink panties, which she had
promptly discarded in the back seat after the incident.
He hesitated before picking them up, enveloped by a
wave of warmth that shot through his brain like a bolt.
It was made of a silky, almost animate material, with
a small black bow embroidered on the front and a
reinforced lining in the crotch. He had already seen
others like it, had already felt the emotion they could
provoke, their extraordinary power of abstraction. He
scrunched it in the palm of his hand, opened his fingers
and was watching it blossom like a flower, release its
scent into his nostrils, when someone tapped on the
glass behind him.
He immediately shoved the undergarment into his
pocket and turned toward the neighbor standing on the
sidewalk, who signaled him to lower his window.
To become an ordinary citizen again, it was not enough
to sort your trash, respect the local customs, keep your
nose clean, pay your taxes. No, it was harder than that,
an unattainable Grail, apparently nothing was ever
enough. Richard, in his place, would no doubt have
smashed the neighbor's face in, but Dan waited for him

to finish while looking elsewhere, the trees, the empty
sky, the man's wife and children returning home in single file, a young cat stalking atop a wall.

I like my city, I pick up my trash, the dentist concluded.

At the same instant, Dan's phone rang in his pocket.

Oh, excuse me a moment, he said, taking the call.

Nath was ringing from the hospital. Mona had gone
into anaphylactic shock when they got home, because of
her wasp sting. They'd had the fright of their lives but
it was all okay now, they were just keeping her under
observation for a few more hours.

Just one thing, though, the cops have taken Richard
away, she added.

He didn't answer, but bent forward with a grimace as if
someone had punched him in the stomach.

When he arrived at the hospital and went to Reception
to ask for Mona's room, he was treated to a disdainful
glance from the duty nurse.

Are you another nutjob, she asked distrustfully.

No, not that I know of, he said.

Nath was leafing through a magazine that she rested
on her knees when he walked in. She put a finger to
her lips and indicated that Mona was asleep. They went
out to the hallway and he briefly hugged her. She was
pale, tired, happy he was there. They headed over to
the coffee machine while she reassured him again about
Mona's condition: according to the intern on call, she'd
merely suffered a large local reaction. But it never failed,

she sighed, Richard still managed to get into it with
him and things turned ugly, it had to come out one way
or another. I'll spare you the details, she said with an
evasive gesture. And how'd it go with the two of you,
everything okay.

We didn't stay out late. We were beat.

She didn't try to find out any more, visibly uninterested.
In fact, she had other things on her mind. She hadn't
gotten rid of Vincent, who refused to move on—the
jerk was still bombarding her with texts that alternated
between pleas and threats, which she didn't answer, and
had outdone himself over the last few hours, a regular
avalanche. It was really getting worrisome. She even
wondered, after not getting a wink of sleep even though
her daughter was out of danger, whether she should
confide in Dan to get his thoughts. She couldn't make
up her mind. She had absolute confidence in him. Or at
least, up to a certain point. She knew he'd cut off an arm
for her. But for Richard, he'd cut off both.

Mona opened one eye when they returned to her room.
She stared at Dan for a few seconds and declared she
was hungry. Her face was a bit puffy. Yeah, okay, let's
see what *you'd* look like, she said.

He went back into the hallway to let her get dressed. He
noticed a laundry bin near the window overlooking the
parking lot and briefly flirted with the idea of chucking
in Marlene's panties, which reminded him of their presence whenever he dug his hand into his pocket—like

81

several minutes earlier, when he wanted change for the coffee machine. The Alfa was parked down below, in the shadow of a bamboo partition covered with two-toned climbing ivy. In the distance, past the army barracks, you could see the twinkling of the pond and the skeleton of an old wind pump repurposed into a diving platform.

They hadn't intended to dawdle, but Mona felt like a burger, and as they didn't want to refuse her after her brush with death, they stopped off at the bowling alley cafeteria and watched with patience and indulgence as she wolfed down her food.

Two mistakes. The first was the choice of venue, given that as far as the owner was concerned, there was no such thing as off-hours when it came to serving the business that one was lucky to work for, especially if one wasn't management. He knew this. He knew it, but like the others he hoped he could run between the raindrops, and so frequented the place much too often, given the lack of better distractions.

So, how was your date, Mona asked, mouth half full, shooting him a look from underneath.

Nath had left the table to take a call from Richard, who was finally resurfacing, and it was no doubt the moment Mona had been waiting for to pop her question.

What date, what are you talking about, he groused. We went to the movies. I don't call that a date. Don't muddle things up.

Oh, call it what you like, I don't care. So how was your movie, tell me.

He looked at her a moment and took a deep breath.

All right, here goes, he announced. We started by doing it in the front seat. Not very practical, but manageable. Then we moved onto the back seat. Then I got the bright idea to lower the seat backs and we started up all over again, like animals. And don't forget that the film lasts more than two hours.

She shrugged. She asked if he thought he was being funny.

I'm not trying to be funny, he answered.

The second mistake was going off with the guy who had come looking for him about a problem with a pinsetter drive chain that was running slack and threatening to snap.

At least it let him cut short this stupid conversation with an eighteen-year-old girl whose godfather he was and whom he had bounced on his knee. He stood up without a moment's hesitation and crossed the cafeteria. Feeling grumpy, he stopped at the bar for a drink, which he considered necessary after the morning's events. From the sound of it, there was no urgency. A few bowls, some laughs drifting over from the lanes.

He recognized the woman's. He downed his drink in one gulp and sat there thoughtfully for a few seconds while the woman continued to giggle.

Marlene stopped laughing when she saw him coming.
A young dude was holding her close, vaguely occupied
with teaching her the rudiments of the game—although
he apparently had another game in mind, especially
since she seemed relatively amenable.

Dan continued on his way as she called after him and
slipped out of her partner's embrace to go join him.
She gave him a large, embarrassed smile, her cheeks
flushed.

I thought, well, I thought you'd call me, she stammered.
Don't worry about me, I just came to fix something, he
said. I think somebody's waiting for you.

She glanced briefly at the young dude who was caught
short and visibly crumbling not far away.

Dan, let's get out of here, she said.

Mona's with me. Go finish your game.

Please, she insisted, lowering her eyes.

You're pretty thickheaded, he said, walking away; then
he retraced his steps and discreetly gave her back her
panties without another word.

Later he saw her again, sitting with Mona, Nath, and
Richard, who were waiting. The latter was recounting
a hornet attack they'd suffered in Yemen during the
extraction of pilots who had bailed out in the mountains
and he called on Dan to back him up.

Telling the same stories over and over, wearing them
down to the nub, puffing them up, trading them, rumi-
nating them among themselves was one of a veteran's

main occupations and you just had to go with it. Two or three guys had drawn closer to listen to Richard while Dan nodded, taking care not to make eye contact with Marlene, who stared at him almost constantly. He needed to pee but held it in, afraid she'd follow him when he had nothing to say to her. He just wanted to go home and put everything back in its place, throw his sheets in the laundry, and trim his hedges.

The afternoon progressed, the sky took on lilac hues. He was now wondering how he'd manage to avoid bringing her home when everyone stood up, but she announced that she thought she'd stick around a bit longer, and since Richard had gotten his car back, Nath offered to let her sister have hers until the next morning. And so, he said to himself, having found his smile, you should never lose hope, never think all is lost.

Trimming his hedges took him a good hour, when others would have needed twice as long, but he was behind on his exercising and he dove into the operation with liberating ardor and intense concentration, sweating blood and water while evacuating all sorts of inopportune thoughts, worrisome reflections, insidious images; and when he examined the result of his labors, blinking and mopping his brow, exhausted, his T-shirt soaked, covered head to foot in vegetal dust and crumbs, not a single goddam leaf stuck out, not a single goddam shrub was out of line. To the point where the dentist began whistling from his yard.

Holy cow, Dan, that's some nice work. How much would you take me for to do mine.

Nothing.

What do you mean, nothing.

I mean nothing, not a cent.

Great. In that case, I'll trade you a cleaning.

He wife had come outside behind him, a slightly chalky blonde who seemed to be shivering internally and whose voice he'd never heard. She gave him an imperceptible nod, head lowered.

By now, day was waning. Dan gathered up the detritus and compacted it in bags, crimped shut the last one at dusk. He took a shower, then spent another good moment tidying up the bedroom, which he inspected with a final glance before going outside, glass in hand, pleased with his accomplishment. The moon had risen, the air was thick with the aroma of freshly cut grass, the hedge shone in ecstatic suffering, there reigned an absolute calm. He was about to light a cigarette when, distractedly surveying his immediate surroundings, his blood froze. He nearly choked when he discovered Nath's car parked a bit farther up the street, lights off.

Marlene. Marlene, of course. But what could that woman have in her noggin, he wondered, approaching the target with the stealth of a Sioux, furtive and bent over despite the darkness.

Taken by surprise, she jumped when he slid in beside her.

What the hell are you doing here, he said, grabbing her arm. What is this, some kind of joke.

You scared me. You're hurting me.

He let go, irritated, without taking his eyes off her. You can't do this, you hear me. You can't just show up like this, goddammit.

At those words, she turned into a rag doll and slumped over in her seat. Her head banged against the steering wheel.

When she came to a few minutes later, she was in his house, lying on the living room couch that was still in shadow. The drapes had been carefully drawn shut. She heard him moving utensils about. She put one foot on the ground and tried to stand, a bit unsteadily. For an instant, she saw a herd of zebras scampering away in a cloud of yellow sand like gold dust.

Feeling better, he asked in a neutral voice, framed in the lit rectangle of the kitchen doorway. Have to get used to your thing there. I've made coffee.

I'll be going.

What difference will five more minutes make. Sit down. You wouldn't want the same thing to happen again.

Barely recovered, she hesitated, looked around her, then obeyed while he set the coffee on the low table and sat down next to her.

I'm so sorry.

You take sugar.

No, thank you.

The atmosphere wasn't great, but the tension had dropped.

I'm really sorry. I feel so ridiculous.

You have to understand one thing, he said, leaving the sentence unfinished.

Excuse me, which way's the bathroom.

He stood up and went to the window, waiting for her to return. With one finger, he pulled the curtains apart a couple of inches and cast an eye outside. All in all, he wasn't too worried, it was highly unlikely anyone had seen them: she wasn't very heavy, he had run hunched over, it had lasted barely ten seconds, a cloud had passed in front of the moon.

They took their seats. You have to understand one thing, he resumed.

Dan, please forgive me. I'm so sorry.

Drink it while it's hot. Should I turn the heat up. You're sure you're okay.

Yes, it was the emotion.

Listen. It's not you. It's me.

No. It's me. I know it. Everything I do is wrong. You see what I mean. You're angry.

I'm not angry. I'm just not much fun, that's all. I've set rules for myself. Drink your coffee.

She did so, watching him over the rim.

I respect that, she said. The need for self-preservation.

I'm so mad at myself for having imposed, if only you

knew. I've ruined everything. Will it bother you if I
smoke. I think I could use one. After that, I'll go.
He nodded gently, but mostly for himself. The flame
of the lighter illuminated the scene like a manger in a
Flemish Renaissance painting. He didn't know whether
she'd done it on purpose, whether a terrible priestess
didn't inhabit the heart of most women.
Can I offer you something stronger, he asked.
She shot him her most disarming smile. Yes, Dan, she answered, but you know perfectly well how all this will end.
He stood up as if in a dream to go find some glasses. If
he'd had the slightest idea how all this would end, there's
no doubt he would immediately have sat back down.


## CLOWNS

A few days later, Richard unveiled the fabulous idea he
had in mind. He'd worked it out down to the smallest
details. He'd taken Dan for a drive and after exiting
the highway parked the Alfa in the middle of nowhere,
surrounded by undergrowth that was starting to green
up again and spread all the way to the bare cliffs nearby.
He was certain this would work. Try as Dan might to
persuade him he was out of his mind, that it was nuts to
take those guys for fools, he wouldn't be swayed.
Exasperated, Dan got out of the car and stood a few
yards away, his back turned, fists jammed in his pockets.

So what you're saying is I can't count on you, Richard flung at him, getting out in turn under the blue sky.

You can count on me to tell you what I think of it, that's for sure.

That doesn't answer my question.

Doesn't it.

On the way back, Richard's jaw remained set and he dropped Dan off in front of the bowling alley without so much as a glance.

It was early afternoon and Dan was due at work, but he needed to think, concentrate on what he meant to do about Richard's fucking scheme, and so he went home instead and stayed shut inside until evening, mulling it over.

Ralph and Gisele lived in one of the small, white, indistinguishable prefab houses that had sprouted up like mushrooms in the late eighties, when the banks were loaning out cash hand over fist and screwing everyone. Ralph's was recognizable by the flag of a motorcycle club he used to belong to when he still had his legs; it floated above the entrance door as a reminder of better days.

I've known motherfuckers like that, Ralph said, scratching his cheek, while Gisele nodded. He'd better watch his step.

You gotta stop him doing it, she declared.

Ralph looked at her tenderly and held out his hand. Listen to what she's saying, dude. Couldn't have put it better myself. This woman is the voice of reason. Love you, Gisele. So when's this bullshit supposed to go down. In three days.

Fine, that gives us time. 'Course, I'm not saying he'll thank us for it. Can't say the shithead's getting any smarter with age. Hey, I heard you just now, you came over on a chopper.

Dan shot Gisele a glance.

Oh, come on, give me a break, Ralph fidgeted while they procrastinated. Come on, goddammit, I'm not going to get on my knees and beg. Get out of the way, he grumbled, maneuvering his wheelchair toward the front door. Jesus Christ, I used to love that, at night. Let's go so I can breathe some of that warm spring air.

It was two days before Richard would speak to him again, when Dan showed up with Mona's tickets.

It was almost noon and he'd just gotten up, face dog-tired and eyes bloodshot. He'd opened the door and turned around without a word, leaving Dan at the doorway with the kind of grunt he generally reserved for intruders, door-to-door salesmen, Jehovah's Witnesses, and process servers of any stripe.

You've lost your phone, Dan said, joining him in the sun-drenched kitchen.

Richard planted himself in front of the coffee maker. Why. I'm the one you came to see. You got something to say to me, he muttered without turning around.

Dan pulled up a chair and sat down, tickets in hand.

If I had anything to say to you, it would be to drop the idea. You should listen to me. You don't fuck with guys like that. Not you. Not me. Not anyone. We're out of our depth.

When Richard turned around, he was almost unrecognizable, so red was his face in spots, and white, blotchy white. Not to mention his rictus. Sometimes, when they were in the thick of it, sweat dripping down their garishly painted faces, he wore that same terrifying expression, and Dan was always glad it wasn't aimed at him.

You think I'm dumber than that bunch of morons, you think they scare me.

It won't work. It's bullshit. They'll never buy it. They won't even bother to verify. They'll pop you without so much as word one.

We'll see about that. Well, you won't. You'll be all comfy in your La-Z-Boy smoking your pipe. Shit, I can't fucking believe this.

There was a hint of melancholy, of weariness in that last statement. He spread the flaps of his bathrobe and let himself drop onto a chair on the other side of the Formica table transformed into a puddle of tepid silver.

I'll do it alone. I've made up my mind and I'm not about to change it. Anyway, thanks a lot, I'll never forget your help, he added, leaning toward Dan. No need to tattoo your name on my forearm. And now you're free to leave, *compañero*, no one's keeping you.

Listen, the guy with the Alfa, I checked up on him, I found out a few things. Do you know who that asshole is. Do you know who he works for. You think you can sucker people like that. So just forget about it. Think for a minute. Every scheme, every possible angle, every swindle, he knows them all, that's what he does.

Richard blinked, looking mean.

Do you know what the fuck I do here. How I spend my life. All the pressures I have. Do you know what it means to have rent and bills to pay, two women to take care of, a shitload of debt. You don't know. You think I'm making this up. You think I've got the cash to pay off his car after what happened. I hope you haven't forgotten that little episode, at least. You didn't exactly come to my rescue, as I recall. If you've got a better plan, I'm all ears. But you don't. There isn't one. We're fucked up the ass. They've dumped us like turds. Remember what your bastard dad said to us. He was right. Boys, you're fighting the wrong war. That's what he said. It was your fucking bastard banker father who was right.

Dan started playing with his teaspoon, moving a sugar cube like a slow skiff across the silvery waves.

I figured you'd bust my balls about this, Richard said, but I didn't think you'd let me down. I never thought that could happen.

I have no desire to lay flowers on your grave, okay. But I will if that happens. At least you can count on that.

He stood up, set the tickets on the table. She can call me, he said. Or you take her. I'm starting to get fed up with that movie.

I'm not giving you a ride, went Richard.

It was a difficult moment for Dan. This was the worst they'd ever weathered. They hadn't always seen eye to eye, they'd had their shouting matches, hadn't spoken to each other for days, but this went beyond all that. A bridge had collapsed. And it was far from over. He spent the afternoon at the bowling alley, checking and rechecking with Ralph by phone to make sure everything was set. The first warm days brought customers in, all the lanes were busy, and he had to keep a constant watch on the machinery. The balls slid nonstop into their cages, the pins flew in all directions, exploded without end.

That evening, he sped straight to Marlene's. He decompressed. He smoked a cigarette with her after they'd fucked, then got dressed, feeling much lighter.

It's nice at your place, he said, hopping on one leg to pull on his trousers.

It's furnished, she answered. You sure you have to go.

Sure and certain. I have to be up early tomorrow, I want to get in a run and do my exercises. I'm not being very disciplined these days.

Once outside, in the lit street, he breathed easier. The air was cool. It stung after a while. The sky was wide open and he'd enjoyed the hour they'd spent together. He still wasn't sure about the long term, but he was sleeping better, it did him good to make love with her. They had more or less decided to keep it to themselves for now, no one needed to know, and that slight air of secrecy fit Dan like a glove. No commitment. No play-acting. No hesitation.

She wasn't making demands, and that was fine by him, even essential. The fact that she hadn't asked for anything scored her another point. Dan's phone rang. Mona told him to forget about the movie, and that he could go fuck himself.

She was very fond of her dad. Ralph called soon afterward to let him know they had the shack and that Gisele had managed to procure all the necessaries from the hospital.

Ralph, I don't know what I'd do without you.

And Gisele.

Right, and Gisele. In any case, I'm getting it in the neck.

I can imagine.

When I tell my mother about this, she'll never believe it. She loves him like a son.

How's she doing.

Not bad. It's her head—not much you can do about that. When I talk about you, she knows who you are. She sends her love.

What really scares the shit out of me is getting old.

Yeah. I dunno. You're probably right.

After hanging up, Dan took a good long shower, nice and cold, dried in front of the open window, and was asleep in no time. If he hadn't had a nightmare, he would surely have slept straight through till morning. But he jolted awake screaming and shook in terror for several long minutes; fortunately, he covered his mattress with a rubber sheet and kept his meds and slippers handy.

The last time he'd renewed his prescription, the shrink had said it'll take the time it takes, Dan, I'm not clairvoyant. But give up on the idea of sleeping like a baby. I'm not a magician either.

This kind of crisis left him beat for the entire day. Once more, he bagged his exercises. He straddled his motorcycle and went to visit the shack. It was a nice day, the Moto Guzzi ran like a dream. It was so good that he arrived feeling more or less alive, face paralyzed by the crisp air, the white tracks of dried salt tears spangling his temples.

The place was magnificent, surrounded by greenery, deserted. The shack was a simple fisherman's hut built near the water, with a small wooden dock that stretched onto the lake. It was here that they'd smoked their first cigarettes, then screwed their first girlfriends while listening to music and puffing on joints. It belonged to the father of one of Ralph's cousins, a solitary angler who'd fallen in the lake and drowned. The place's ill-starred reputation kept people away, a moss-covered wooden fence kept it closed, the road leading to it was abandoned. Everyone had grown older since then.

The padlock on the door still worked. He opened the shutters. More than anything, the surrounding trees had grown. The interior was more or less maintained, tidy; there was a bench, a portable stove, a table, a staved-in armchair, a clutch of old fishing rods in a corner, a basket hanging on the wall, a net, storm lamps.

He pulled a blanket from his saddlebags, a few provisions, candles, rolls of cellophane tape, bananas, and brought them inside. Before leaving, he walked out onto the dock. The water lapped below his feet. The silence and surroundings were lovely. Even if you didn't know the first thing about fishing, it still made you feel like going out to buy a rod and some worms.

He was back in town by midmorning. Ralph introduced him to two guys, two brothers, whom they could count on to handle things—and maybe more, if they hit it off, and if Dan could dislodge some extra cash for possible further activities, which he might.

After sending part of his pension to his mother, he was nearly cleaned out, but he promised the guys he'd manage if it turned out he needed to keep them around.

We trust you, buddy, declared one of them, slapping him on the shoulder while the other bro nodded. If Ralph says you're square, you're square.

Dan joined Marlene at the pool between noon and two. They rested a moment in their deck chairs, eyes shut. When he opened his, she was looking at him. Can I tell you something, he asked her after a minute, and as she nodded, he said, your glasses. Marlene, forgive me for saying so, but they don't suit you at all.

Yes, but that's going to change soon, she answered. I'm getting more and more used to contacts.

He dozed off again, mentally rehearsing the operation that, in itself, shouldn't pose any problems, he'd done it dozens of times.

His name is Vincent.

He opened his eyes. Who's that.

The guy Nath is seeing. His name is Vincent. I heard it when they were on the phone. She was talking to him in the back room, and when she came out, she was pale, white with fury. I feel a storm brewing. What, what's with you, as if you didn't know about it.

He was a bit dumbfounded. I didn't think she was seeing *one* guy. I thought she was just having a few *flings*.

Anyway, it's none of our business. You want me to put some lotion on you.

No, no lotion, thanks.

In any case, it's not very reassuring. It doesn't seem to be going very well.

Let's not panic. Your sister knows how to handle herself.

Yeah, but if Richard ever found out.

Please. Let's not talk about worst-case scenarios. Spare me. I'm going to get a headache if we keep on much longer.

At those words, he stood up and dove into the pool. Swam the entire length underwater. Then he lay there, floating on his back.

When he returned to his chair, Marlene picked up the conversation as if nothing had happened.

The one you have to watch out for is Mona. She's the one who told me about it. She never brings it up, but things haven't exactly improved between her and her mother.

He grabbed a magazine and leafed through it distractedly. Yes, but what can we do about it. What's the point of telling me this. As if there was something we could do. Things like this happen in every home, behind every window. I'm going to get some sandwiches, what would you like. Mona wouldn't do that. She wouldn't go that far. Mona's at a difficult age. She seems to have trouble controlling herself. I wouldn't trust her if I were you. When I was a teen, I felt like killing people, I'm just saying. Anyway, get me a veggie.

You know, I warned Nath. I told her she should watch her step. But I guess she thinks she's smarter than everyone else. It seems to run in the family. I don't mean you, Marlene, I don't have any idea. But the rest of them are know-it-alls.

I was wondering what you're doing tonight.

I'm going to hit the sack early. I have to recuperate. I told you I spent a lousy night, and I need some sleep.

You could just come have a drink at my place.

No, it's nice of you to offer, but I'm going to bed.

Dan, it's only two in the afternoon.

You see, I don't even know what I'm saying anymore. Exhaustion.

While everyone else was going nuts, Dan, for his part, was determined to stay the course.

Late that afternoon, he received a text from Mona saying that the date of their tickets was no good and they'd have to pick a later one. He answered that unfortunately Lynch's film would be gone by then. She shot back that she could care less.

Meanwhile, Nath was clipping a poodle. According to her, there was no dog stupider or more annoying, or less worthy of interest, and she was eager to be rid of it. Marlene was trimming the claws of a young cat she had just dewormed, and the radio was murmuring an oldie by Sinatra in the background. When Vincent came in, accompanied by a kind of long-haired mongrel on a leash, she raised her eyes as Nath's clippers slipped from her hands and continued to vibrate on the floor at the end of their cord and the poodle bared its fangs.

Marlene, said Nath, unplugging her machine, would you do me a favor and go buy me some cigarettes, if you don't mind.

Are you sure, asked Marlene, standing up.

I'm sure.

She untied her smock and slipped on a coat while the lights of the shopping center lit up beneath a reddening sky. She crossed the parking lot and hugged the opposite wall, between a clothing boutique of questionable taste and a store for running gear—the people coming out of it looked like clowns, but they examined their kicks with delighted and self-congratulatory faces. From where she stood, she could see Nath and the guy from behind. Breakups: she had lived through her share and always found herself on the wrong side. Score-settling, recriminations, nasty arguments—she'd known it all. Decent men didn't grow on trees. She couldn't hear anything, but Nath was waving her arms and seemed to be shouting, and the aforementioned Vincent was keeping pace. Passersby started slowing down to enjoy the show. Nath shut the curtains.

Marlene had once even known a man who had hit her on the head with a hammer. When Vincent came out, she practically ran to the shop and found Nath in the back room, short of breath, downing a large glass of water.

## CALF

Keeping Richard from doing something boneheaded was one thing. Keeping his financial backers from not liking that he skipped out on them at the last second, with no notice, was something else again.

I thought you'd thought of that, went Ralph, chugging a beer in one gulp.

Maybe we should go see them.

Ralph rubbed the remnants of his thighs with a nervous laugh.

Have you forgotten, he said. Showing up with your white handkerchief. Y'almost got us all killed.

We wiped them all out. I don't want to start that again.

And how'd we get out of it, huh. 'Cause at a certain point, you stopped using your head. At a certain point, you weren't thinking anymore. You shoved that grenade in their faces and if you hadn't, we'd all be dead. See what I mean.

They were at one of those Saturday night rodeos on the edge of town. Motors were growling, beer was in kegs, pills were passed around by the fistful—the guys helped themselves directly from the military infirmary and the girls raided the medicine chests of the women they worked for. The night was cool and sparkling. Dan had pushed Ralph's wheelchair to the top of a hillock and they were admiring the spectacle. The guys bet their shirts and their pensions on the craziest among them, the ones behind the wheel.

Richard made himself a little cash on these evenings, because he was a bit crazier than the rest, a bit more adrenalin-fueled at the starting line. And that, too, was dangerous. The goddam business he'd gotten himself into was proof. Sometimes it seemed he was running on ether.

He'd given Ralph a manly embrace and ignored Dan, who was wondering if they'd ever get past this, if there was any chance they'd come through it intact, whether things between them could ever be the same or whether they would learn what it meant to be alone.

Ralph had brought his drone to film the race and Richard had said I wanna see that, call me, and had turned toward his car counting his cash, end of story.

His mood hadn't changed after the race. He was even looking mighty fit, surrounded by groupies, and Dan watched him walk away with the Alfa guy who had shot him a glance in passing. He was gripping Richard's shoulder and seemed to be congratulating him.

You see what I see, went Dan. Next thing you know, they'll be slipping each other the tongue. Mmm, see if you can get that, just in case.

Way ahead of you, answered Ralph without taking his eyes off the monitor.

Dan suddenly had a burning desire to be elsewhere. Why not between Marlene's thighs, he thought to himself, surprised by the urgency of it.

He grabbed his phone and asked if he could come by later, say around midnight, for that drink she'd mentioned.

Dan, that was yesterday.

Yeah, maybe, I dunno. No. Does it matter.

He showed up at her place at around two in the morning. She was in pajamas. He was bleeding from the forehead, maybe one nostril as well, and was covered in dust. Her hand flew to her mouth and she let him in.

It's fine, I'm all right, he said, entering with heavy steps. It's all fine, it's just part of a plan. But I don't want to talk about it. Nothing for you to worry about. Let me take a shower first, and if you have any bandages.

No, but I'll go out and get some.

Noooo, no need, he called, but he heard the door slam behind her.

When she returned, he was coming out of the bathroom, a towel around his loins. He looked at her for a moment, asked if she'd gone out like that, in her pajamas.

There's nobody out there, she answered. I didn't meet a soul.

As she was in pajamas and he simply wrapped in a bath towel, they collapsed onto the bed without further ado.

You're quite the mystery, she whispered to him during a pause.

Her voice sounded thick. A moment later, he noticed she'd fallen asleep. He frowned at the thought of getting up, getting dressed, going home. There was nothing he needed to do. He felt good right where he was. Whether it was the place, the silence, the relaxation of his muscles, or else the fact that sex with her was getting better and better, who knows. Whatever the case, she was clearly lightening his burden. When he had walked up fast to Richard and the other guy, the backer, he was in a hurry to be with her, to be on top of her, to be done with them.

Richard, stop, he'd blurted in a dark voice, grabbing him roughly by the arm and forcing him to turn around. Everybody's going to be sorry.

Richard had lost no time reacting. The drone had stabilized above their heads, but no one was lifting his eyes to admire the sky. With a violent shove, he'd sent Dan rolling into the bushes. That's where he'd cut his forehead, on a rock jutting from the spiny branches. But he'd gotten up, blood running down his cheek, and come back for more.

You're gonna fuck it up, Richard, he barked. No way you can drive that fast all night long. Shit, just ask your shrink. Your body will crash before you get halfway.

Richard's fist had shot out at stupefying speed and smashed Dan in the cheekbone like a brick. It was still smarting as he slipped from bed where Marlene was sleeping with her hands balled into fists, turned on her side, and he dressed quickly, in silence.

Day was barely breaking when he walked into a cafeteria and swallowed three croissants in a row at the counter, chewing methodically. He was the only customer. An old geezer, stooped and pallid, was washing the floor behind him with a microfiber squeegee mop that Dan had been using for some time and with which he was mighty pleased. Sports scores that meant nothing to him paraded across a screen. Another guy was making sandwiches in the rear kitchen, rubbing his eyes and yawning. The fog slowly dissipated on the horizon, broke up under an empty sky gone mauve.

Arriving home in the first light of dawn, he found Nath cooling her heels in front of his place. He said nothing, parked the car, nervously yanked the hand brake.

Dan, I have to talk to you, she said. Where were you.

You're parked on the wrong side of the street, but whatever. Let's go inside.

She tossed her bag on the bench while he rushed into the bathroom to wash his hands and check his bandage.

What happened to you, she asked from outside the door.

Nothing special. And what about you. What's going on.

For a minute she stared at the tips of her shoes. Above the sink, bent over, his face was turned toward her, the tap was running, a few droplets of water splashed over the side.

I know you won't like this, she sighed, but listen, Dan, I'm in big trouble.

No kidding. Otherwise you wouldn't be at my door at seven in the morning looking like the ragged end of nowhere.

He knew the story, Marlene had told him the whole thing in detail, but he let her talk, took the opportunity to think.

At the end, he shook his head. How'd you manage to get yourself in such a mess. You really are a little kid, this is crazy.

I was tired of my yoga classes. I was tired of a lot of
things. I didn't pay attention.

She helped him apply his bandage properly.

So now what do we do, he asked. Tell me how you plan
to put out the fire. What have you got in mind.

I don't know. But who's gonna help me if you don't.

He went to open the curtains and shutters. It was bright
daylight outside now. He stood for a few moments in
front of the window. The dentist was walking his dog.
Noticing Dan, he signaled that his hedges were waiting and mimed a guy brushing his teeth. As he put on
his gloves on his porch, he called out, by the end of the
week, Dan, you think you can do that.

Dan nodded and shut the window with a grimace. He
turned to Nath.

I'll start by having a word with him, he said. That's
what you want, right.

He knows I'm married and don't want to see him
anymore. He couldn't give a flying fuck. He showed
up with his horrible mutt. And what about tomorrow.
He'll pound on my door and Richard will answer and
what happens then. Richard's a bundle of nerves at the
moment. What's the matter with him.

Dan shrugged. I think he gets panic attacks. He doesn't
talk about it. I hardly saw him last night. I hung out
with Ralph.

It was like he'd been bitten by a rabid dog, when he
came home. I went straight to bed.

That's the best thing to do, with him. No sense trying to talk about it when he's like that. Maybe I should take him to the country for a few days so he can chill out. I could take him camping, the weather's warming up. It'd do us good, him *and* me. It always gets us back on our feet. Every time.

As soon as she'd left, he stripped off his clothes, which he tossed in the laundry basket, and pulled on a pair of shorts. Then he sat on his rowing machine to conquer the twelve miles he planned to supplement with a few rounds at the punching bag and some planks, after which he could finally take a shower, give himself a once-over with the loofah mitt.

Somewhere, and despite the challenges facing him, he was glad about the part he'd have to play to get Richard and Nath out of the mess they'd each gotten themselves into. At least he felt useful again, at least he felt he could do that. Safeguarding Richard's life during all those years when they'd slaved to get by was the only thing that kept him going, a sufficient, redemptive reason that gave meaning to his own life, and it was good to play this part again, to feel his spirit merging with his body. The clock chimed ten. He had plenty of time to go see Ralph before checking in at the bowling alley. For a second, he'd been surprised to notice his bed wasn't slept in. It was as if everything was trying to take on a strange coloration, like that night in Chechnya when the colors turned phosphorescent—he'd told Richard he was having hallucinations, was going crazy, and then at dawn it had all dissipated, he'd simply had a bad case of the runs. He cast a last glance at the living room, where he had shaken and plumped up the cushions, everything in order. He washed his hands before going out and took the car rather than his bike so as not to tempt Ralph. Clock's ticking, the latter declared in the middle of a haircut, the regulation three centimeters. That's why I'm sprucing myself up. Say hi to Gisele.

They hugged. He liked Gisele well enough, but she was almost always in a white smock and carried a vague odor of hospital around her. Ralph thought so too, but he felt a morbid desire for her that excited him way beyond reason.

How are you feeling, he asked, rubbing a hand over the silky rug that covered his skull.

Fine.

I've got some Red Bull in the fridge.

Dan stretched, cracked his knuckles. I'll have to re-member to share my music with him, he sighed. So he can have something to listen to. It should calm him down when he wakes up. I'm thinking the complete Johnny Cash. On missions, that's all he listened to. And Metallica.

Good thing it's not winter. He'd've frozen his ass off out there.

No, spring is perfect. I hope we'll have rain, for the growing season, but later is better. I checked the forecast for the next two weeks on WeatherPro, we should be okay.

Those things are a scam.

It's not a scam. I get radar images in real time. You gotta live in the present.

Yeah. Anyway, we're ready.

I'll call you.

We'll be around.

At noon, as Dan wasn't hungry, he went straight to work, spraying deodorant in the shoes, wiping down the pins, removing oil stains from the bowling balls and treating them with ball cleaner. There was a tightness in his gut. Despite previous experience, there was no getting around it: this was the unpleasant phase, when the mind, in a fit of sheer lucidity, spun full throttle and gave you heartburn. He thought about Richard, everything they'd been through together, and his heartburn only grew worse. He swallowed a tablet to neutralize his proton pump.

Then came the phase of painful stupefaction that left you completely disoriented, wandering, like being caught outdoors on a stormy night. He looked at the time. He got to his feet with a grimace, took off his overalls, dressed, and went up to Brigitte's office to tell her he was going home because of a bad stomach flu. She was wearing a flowered blouse, with rouge on her cheeks and filed nails. She didn't give him a hard time. Don't forget to wash your hands often, she advised.

The third phase was triggered as he was heading toward his car, blinded by the dazzling sun, assailed by the smell of waffles. In Iraq, he had taken a bullet in the calf but kept running like crazy for several hundred yards. That was phase number three. The one that galvanized, obliterated everything. The one where you no longer felt anything at all, where thinking stopped, where nothing else mattered, where you jumped calmly out of the trenches, fuse windward, under a torrent of machine-gun fire.

## CLOCKWORK

Dan sat at the kitchen table, hands between his knees, not reacting. Richard was preparing a thermos of coffee and insulting him profusely, but Dan wasn't listening. He was staring into space, and Richard took his silence and lowered head for contrition—which did nothing to lessen the rage and contempt Dan inspired in him. The words fucking asshole recurred often in Richard's full-frontal litany.

Outside, daylight waned in the camellias.

Got anything to say for yourself, you fucking asshole, Richard was badgering him just as the back door nearly flew off its hinges and two hulking brutes came crashing in, throwing themselves on Richard in a single motion and tackling him to the ground while Dan jumped up, knocking over his chair, and dove into the fray to immobilize Richard, who bellowed and struggled like a man possessed.

Gisele leaned over him and said calm down, Richard, you're among friends, before slapping a wide strip of adhesive tape over his mouth and jabbing a syringe into his thigh. The image that flitted across Dan's mind at that instant was of a calf being branded with a red-hot iron, minus the smoke.

It won't take long, said Gisele as she turned toward Ralph in the doorway and gave him a thumbs-up that everything had gone swimmingly, while the other two trussed Richard up like a sausage and he went slack. When his eyes closed, they carted him off in the van waiting near the yard. Gisele took the wheel. Dusk was falling and Dan had heard enough to feel a vague melancholy the rest of the trip.

You're doing it for his own good, said Ralph, gripping his wheelchair on the sharp turns. Don't forget that. Dan shook his head. The game was far from over. They arrived at the shack in late afternoon, after the two brothers. The sky was turning orange over the woods and gilded the small lake where the cousin's dad had drowned. They carried Richard inside gently—or as gently as the two young guys were able—while Dan pissed against a tree in the warm air. You could already hear an owl. Before leaving, he took a moment to make sure everything was okay. They had spread a blanket over

Richard; the two hulks were playing jacks. He congratulated them on how smoothly the operation had gone and they bumped fists, linked fingers. Tell him I'll be back tomorrow night. If he gets too rowdy, throw a bucket of water on him. They bumped fists again.

Gisele had made him a bag of sandwiches. She'd added some California dates, trail mix, and protein bars for the return trip.

She's amazing, she thinks of everything, Ralph said in delight as he accompanied Dan to his car. I dream about having legs and carrying her on my back.

Now that's serious.

Ralph handed him the keys. They've filled her up, checked the oil and tires, and loaded the trunk with bottled water. Those boys know what they're doing.

They hugged briefly. Ralph had lost his legs, but he still had a pair of arms that were solid as oak.

Half an hour later, Dan was back in town.

He wasn't sure what to expect. You could never really know. He imagined facing foulmouthed louts who'd give him the fish-eye and a hard time. Among that crowd, you had to get up pretty early to find guys who were more suspicious and less accommodating.

But that's not how it played out. Jacky, the guy with the Alfa, was about to plunge his little nephew in a bathtub full of ice and Dan told him it wouldn't do any good.

There were also two young women, one of whom was trying to reach a doctor and the other was chewing gum. Jacky was holding the red, trembling baby in his arms and was about to lose his shit.

Give him sugar water, Dan barked. Don't let him get too uncovered and keep his room aired out.

The three of them seemed so clueless that they followed his orders without question, in a frenzy.

I'm filling in for Richard, Dan announced.

All things considered, Jacky wasn't such a mean bastard, and this new, bewildering situation had left him so unsettled that he ended up agreeing to the solution Dan proposed. But on one condition, since it wasn't like the parties exactly trusted one another, and that was that Dan take along Julia, the girl with the chewing gum, to keep an eye on him.

At which Jacky had given the girl a questioning look. She'd answered that it was all the same to her, and Dan, looking at her, had concluded that pretty much everything was all the same to her, or else it was just her manner.

When they were ready to leave, the baby seemed to have fallen asleep and its mother gave a weak smile.

Pain in the ass, that narcolepsy business, Jacky groused.

He smashed into a tree a few months ago, said Dan. It's like I was trying to tell you, Richard has a serious handicap. I wouldn't wish it on anybody. Of course, Churchill was narcoleptic and it didn't slow him down, back when he was young. But he didn't drive.

The night was black and the stars shining when they left town. Dan hit the gas. If he was to get there by dawn, no time to drag their heels.

You can floor it, Julia said. I'm not a nervous passenger.

So much the better. He turned on his radar detector—a gift from Richard, pale quirk of fate—and burned asphalt while Julia dug into a pastrami sandwich. Though Dan hadn't protested, he'd resented having a passenger foisted on him, preferring his solitude. But his opinion was starting to change. Having company could help him avoid boredom, stay alert.

Don't take it personally, but I don't like talking much, she said.

Did I say anything, he answered.

Stop when you can. I have to pee.

He halted on the shoulder. There was very little traffic. It was still early to be stretching his legs, but he felt like a breather and took a few steps in the dark. He had learned that when everything was going too well, be careful. They were still a long way from bowling a strike. The first pins were down and out. There were others. From *The Art of War*, he had retained that the true problem solver does so before the problems occur, and clearly this wasn't his case. He heard her urinating in the bushes. He sent a text to Ralph to let him know everything was copacetic.

While she was pulling her pants back up, he saw a camper that he'd zipped past a good while before.

Annoyed, he gave two or three horn blasts that ripped through the night.

Terrific, she snickered as she came back. Great way not to attract attention.

He peeled off without answering; they didn't say a word for another fifteen minutes and Dan concentrated on his driving, flying along the road. His thoughts didn't take him very far. Traffic intensified as they approached a large urban area and he had to slalom among the sleepers and the barely awake, passing RVs and trucks, taking the endless ring road that forced him into a ten-mile detour: the clowns who'd designed this layout deserved to be flayed alive.

By the time they finally got out of the suburbs bathing in the splendor of HPS lights and were back under the black sky, the remaining trickle of nocturnal travelers having faded into the landscape, Julia had eaten all of Gisele's sandwiches.

He pulled his hand from the empty paper bag he'd just explored thoroughly and shot her a look. She had put on her headphones. Now and then she sang along in a loud voice to music he couldn't hear.

He stopped at a service station. I thought we were in a hurry, she said when he retook his seat next to her with a bag of provisions. He looked at his watch. He unfolded a map on his knees and bit into a ham and cheese sandwich while checking the route. He was about to say something when he started chewing air, then had

trouble swallowing. He felt a kind of plaster cast glued
to his palate that he couldn't dislodge. He had to stick
in his fingers and spit the amalgamation into a paper
napkin.

That was gross, she said.

He got back on the road, drinking water from a plastic
bottle.

He drove fast, cold, lighting the lanes with his repeated
high-beam signals.

What do you do, for a living.

Temp work, she answered.

They sped through plains, over rivers and streams,
climbed hills and cliffs. He regularly had to activate the
wipers because of the insects and moths that splattered
against their windshield.

She snorted. Who are you fooling that you're doing this
for free. Are you fucking kidding me.

What about you. What do you do it for.

She became lost for a moment in contemplating the
emptiness, then suddenly shrugged. Who knows. I don't
have any long-term plans. I'm here, but I could just as
easily be somewhere else. What diff.

He nodded gently.

Richard and I grew up together, we were never apart, he
said, looking pensive. We've been through it all. Yeah,
I wouldn't do this for anybody else, I wouldn't touch a
scene like this with a ten-foot pole, if not for him. I don't
want any trouble.

By the way, I'm a dyke. Just letting you know.

You can be whatever you want, doesn't matter to me.

I'm in a shitty relationship at the moment. Don't hold it against me. I want to give myself time to figure shit out, but I never can. My parents cut me off—cool of them, don't you think.

Try to get some sleep, he said.

He lifted his foot as they approached a radar gun, distractedly fingering the back of his neck.

It would be good if we could stop for a minute, she said, avoiding his gaze.

They had barely gone halfway. It wasn't as if she'd drunk a lot; she must have had a bladder like a bird's or acute cystitis. He took advantage to stretch his legs again. The farther north they went, the chillier the night became, but it was invigorating, made the blood circulate. He had two messages, one from Marlene asking where he'd disappeared to and one from Ralph about Richard, who had woken up, who they still weren't ready to untie, and who, he added, was busting their eardrums and their balls.

He shut his phone when Julia returned, shivering loudly. Then, as she became curious and started to press, he finally showed her a photo of the gang of them together and she pointed at Marlene, asking if that was his girlfriend, and he shook his head.

No, of course not, what makes you say that.

They way she's looking at you.

He scoffed. Ha ha, that's a good one, but no, sorry, I don't have a girlfriend. And lucky for her. I'm a prime example of the guy who's impossible to live with. I'm really a poisoned present. I don't like going out and I get up three times a night.

Seeing that she kept silent, he peeled back onto the road.

It was one in the morning and they whipped through the darkness that was only slightly pierced by the wan light of the dashboard.

No way. Your father was a banker. I don't believe you.

It made her laugh, that banker business—it made a lot of people laugh, and yet it was the truth.

Yeah, except the asshole got wiped out in the crash and had a heart attack. That's why I'm not rich. He only left us the house, that's where I live now, my mother's in hospice and it's okay.

He shut up when he noticed she'd fallen asleep.

I'm not sleeping, she said. I'm pretending to be asleep. But it's not exactly toasty, can you turn up the heat.

Yeah, but you'd be better off sleeping for real, we still have a ways to go.

He filled up the tank again. He liked his car, but it guzzled, especially when driven flat out.

He woke Julia when they made the swap, at seven sharp. The guy was on time. Dawn was just breaking, forming iridescent patterns in the fuel puddles on the surface of a ditch where they drained the boats. They decanted the bags without a word, just a nod on either side, and that was that.

Dan was amazed. From the start, the whole thing had gone like clockwork, not a single hitch, no nasty surprises. It was as if a good fairy had taken an interest. On the return trip, he drove for two hours and pulled over to take a nap.

She shook him awake. I let you sleep for fifteen minutes, but we've got to get moving, can't hang around here too long.

He stepped out of the car and poured a bottle of mineral water over his head. It was already midmorning, sunny, birds were flying above the green trees, farmers tending the fields, cows wandering around a prairie. Rubbing his head with a towel, he thought about the half-baked scheme Richard had cooked up, the tears of blood they might have shed, and he congratulated himself on setting things right.

Later, after verifying the goods, Jacky pronounced that all was cool, and that he liked that, liked a job well done, guys who did things by the book and could drive fast. Dan could barely stand on his feet after twenty-four solid hours at the wheel, and now that the tension was falling, that his arms and legs weighed a ton, he could only manage a weak smile when they told him the baby's fever had dropped and was doing great thanks to him and his brilliant suggestions.

Tell Richard we're all square, Jacky whispered to him in the doorway. But from now on, I'll have to do without his services. No choice. I've got a family too.

Dan looked around for Julia before leaving, but she had returned to the sofa and was chewing her gum, looking away.

A walk in the park. After the hallucinatory stretch he'd gone through, that was the only term for a simple half hour of driving calmly down a quiet, pretty road.

Even rolling at thirty miles an hour, meeting no one, no houses, no lights, he zigzagged like a drunk—even though he'd declined a drink at Jacky's and hadn't taken any uppers since the night before—lurching forward, botching easy curves. It was fatigue, extreme fatigue. The near impossibility of keeping his teary, bloodshot eyes open.

With a start, just as he was about to face-plant on the steering wheel, he braked sharply and leaped from the car, roaring to wake the dead, jumping up and down, slapping his face and thighs, shadowboxing. He reached toward one of the car's fenders, gathered up a few drops of dew in the hollow of his palm and rubbed it over his face. It even tasted good.

Whatever the case, he started up again on a better footing and finally the shack appeared among the branches. A fire was burning. It was ten-thirty; it had taken him more than an hour. He knew fatigue made you less sensitive to pain, and that was the silver lining. He got out to open the gate and when he climbed back in the car, he noticed his finger was bleeding. He hadn't felt a thing. Sucking it, he told himself he was in the best possible shape for confronting Richard—better than rolling up into a ball.

They were sitting around a fire. Ralph raised his arm on seeing him come up. Shit, man, he did it, he bellowed. Come here for a hug, you son of a bitch.

The fire was crackling, shooting out sparks and dancing on the lake.

Man, you should've seen the row he kicked up, the shit he said. He even tried to bite us, ask Gisele.

I had to put in earplugs, she said.

He calmed down at daybreak, Ralph continued, and had coffee. He said he had some shit to settle with you. We can stick around if you like.

The two brothers looked at him, grinning.

No, go get some sleep, said Dan. I'll take over.

They stacked more wood on the fire before leaving. The brothers skipped stones over the lake while Dan exchanged a few more words and hugs with the other two. Anyway, you'll see, we've left him tied up, Ralph concluded. Watch yourself, but you know all that.

He waited for the van to drive away, silence to return—one of those staggeringly majestic silences that only occur in the middle of nature—and, after wondering whether he should bring something, some alcohol or cigarettes or treats that were still lying on the back seat, he showed up empty-handed, features drawn, zombie-like, ready to suffer Richard's bad mood.

Seeing Dan framed in the doorway, Richard let out a dull grunt. He was sitting on the floor, bound hand and foot, green with rage. You'll pay for this, he hissed between gritted teeth. They exchanged dark looks, then Dan turned around and shut the door behind him. Richard's curses immediately grew distant, their message largely muffled, then abruptly stopped before Dan had even squatted near the fire. Gisele had left him a thermos of coffee and some biscuits in a Tupperware container that he was supposed to return to her when he and Richard were done. He wasn't hungry but his stomach was empty and he munched them one by one, without appetite. The coffee, on the other hand, was a godsend. He thought sadly of Nath's, which was thick, contraindicated for heart cases, and absolutely black.

Can we talk now, or do I turn around and leave, he asked, standing near the door.

Untie me.

I've just covered twelve hundred miles, I'm dead on my feet, and I'm not going to fight with you.

You'll see. Untie me, for Christ's sake.

Okay, let's get some air.

He untied only his legs, helped him stand. Barely on his feet, Richard tried to give him a kick that ended its trajectory in empty space.

For an instant, they stood glaring at each other.

I'm not expecting any thanks, said Dan, but let's try moving on to something else. Either that or I'm going to bed.

If he'd known their argument would last until daybreak, that climbing back up that hill would be so hard, he would have brought a chair: Richard could really hold a grudge, and making him see that Dan had acted in his interest long remained an unattainable goal, a star so distant that it blinked only intermittently.

In the gray dawn, as the last of the logs burned out, they shared a few beers and bananas and agreed to go camping here when they felt better, when the final traces of their quarrel had fizzled.

You can drive, said Dan, handing him the keys.

A gorgeous mirror carp leaped out of the water, then vanished with a splash.

Did that fish smile at me or am I dreaming, thought Dan, bug-eyed.

He returned home in early morning. He heard a voice saying, so, young Dan, back from your trip, I see.

His heart skipped a beat. Before even lifting his eyes to the dentist, he became aware of his disheveled looks, his three-day scruff, his graveyard pallor, his ash-covered shoes—he'd made sure the fire was out while Richard gathered up the banana peels and wrappers—and he stepped into the shade. The other blinked in the dazzling sunlight. Dan patted for his keys. Say, the dentist continued in a firmer tone, I hope you haven't forgotten.

His stupid dog was barking for no reason.

Never fear, Dan answered. It's etched in my brain.

Once inside, finally alone, in peace, an enormous weight lifted off him, he could practically have shed tears of joy. He wiped his cheeks with his sleeve and downed a few sleeping pills just in case—his brutal nightmares could return even after two sleepless nights, or after a marathon. Then he locked his door, unplugged his phone, and got into bed without even washing, neglecting to brush his teeth. In the dark, he listened to his messages. There were enough from Marlene to choke a horse.

## DREAMS

Nath was losing sleep over the thought that Vincent might never go away. The poor boy was a ticking time bomb. Nath woke up worried and went to bed anxious—it couldn't go on. She was in danger of giving herself away, somehow letting the cat out of the bag, forgetting a detail, talking in her sleep.

He was becoming so clingy. She'd been weak enough to let him stay one evening after closing time because he claimed he was going crazy, was going to kill himself if he could no longer smell her, touch her, lick her breasts, etc., and she'd felt pity, her female heart had taken pity on him, she had let him come in and had given herself to him on the table where they treated the animals, and he had knocked over a tub of shampoo that had made the floor slippery and she had started to come violently, to tremble, without really being able to identify the cause of that long tremor that coursed through her body, the kind that happened so rarely, but the fact was, now she was paying the price for her slip, she should never have done that, she had lost her head, and she had gotten home late, cheeks on fire, and had benefited from an incredible stroke of luck because Richard wasn't back yet. Dan had promised to take care of it and she was waiting for him in a local bar.

She had had only a few inconsequential dalliances in eighteen years of marriage and had never encountered this kind of problem; the guys faded away at daybreak and she forgot their names a moment later. It was simple and easy. With Vincent, it was neither.

Dan arrived bang on time. It was nice out, April was making with some truly glorious days and he pulled up a chair in the sun.

I don't want you to hurt him, she said.

What exactly do you want me to do. I promised to trim that moron's hedges, which'll keep me busy all weekend. And I'm taking Mona to see *Pride and Prejudice*. I loved the book.

I want you to tell him to be sensible, that I'm a married woman and I have a life. Tell him I love my husband, that's all you have to say. Tell him I love my husband. That I'd like us to part as friends.

Should be okay. I'll try to find a moment. I doubt it'll take long. Unless he gets pissy with me.

He won't. You're a head taller than he is.

And I've learned how to kill.

Oh, and also tell him not to bring in his dog anymore. There are other grooming salons. He just stands there staring at me, and the other clients stare at him, and half those women are spiteful and pregnant to the eyeballs and then they stare at me.

You know, some small guys are stronger than tall ones. But got it, no more dog.

I will say he's pretty fit, not an ounce of fat on him. I forgot about yoga. He can't wait for me after class anymore, not even on the corner. Especially when I'm with a girlfriend.

I'll have him tie a string around his finger.

Talk to him. Tell him what you have to say calmly. He doesn't listen to me because I'm a woman. You he'll listen to. Just scare him a little, like when you don't smile.

Watching Dan head off, she reflected that she and Richard had tried to marry him off half a dozen times before giving up and that he'd make a good husband if he weren't such a loner, if there weren't that double-bolted door way down inside him.

She found Marlene in the salon, in her underwear in the back room. She was about to put on her smock and was examining herself in profile in the full-length mirror. You can still get by, but it's starting to show, Nath told her. Put on your glasses.

She had a new pair, round with fine steel rims that looked pretty good on her, according to most people, but they must not have been in her prescription and they left her blinded to the obvious. Still, arguing got you nowhere, thought Nath with a resigned shrug. They just had to wait—sooner or later, whether Marlene liked it or not, she wouldn't be able to hide it any longer.

The latter put on her smock and examined herself again in the mirror, tightened the garment, inspected her profile. Really, there's no rush, she declared. Let me breathe. I'm just starting to feel at home here, with all of you. I hadn't felt that way in a long time. And it's all thanks to you, it's wonderful, you don't know how badly I needed that.

An old surge of affection for her impossible sister rose in Nath's heart, and she gave a hint of a smile.

I'm glad you're here too. I wasn't sure, you know. I wondered if you could get used to the climate, the atmosphere, the locals, all of it, because it's a bit peculiar here, a little closed off, if you know what I mean. One could just as easily not like it, it's not always a barrel of laughs, there's that stench of war and muted anxiety that's never far away, you have to get used to it, but

you've adapted well, everyone loves you, me first and
foremost, you know that, you know me, I'm not always
in the best mood, you know me, she said, putting on her
outfit as well.

She sometimes wondered if she'd been too hard on her
sister in the past. But she didn't forget that Marlene had
also asked for it.

She grabbed a cat in its cage and started cleaning its ears
while Marlene took out the tools and products for sale.
At the idea that Dan would take things in hand, Nath
felt reassured, a tiny bit regretful but calmer, and when
her eyes again fell on her sister who was quietly flipping
through the appointment book—daylight haloed her
in a lovely powdery copper—she felt closer to Marlene
than she would have expected.

She wasn't displeased. It was a good thing, wasn't it. It
was fun having a sister. Not a daughter, not a friend, but
a sister. For a while, she had completely forgotten about
this bond. There had been a few hiccups at first. Marlene
had arrived like the proverbial bull in a china shop, it
had been hard going for at least two months, but there,
that morning, oblivious to the cat whining in her hands,
she felt a soft, warm rain on her head, as if a soap bubble
had burst over her.

And so she ended up saying, you know, that guy, yeah,
the one with the dog, you must have wondered, well
yes, he's the one, there, I'm getting rid of him, so that's
it, you've been taken into my confidence, so be super

careful, darling, you don't know anything, aren't aware of anything, haven't seen or heard anything.

You called me darling.

Yes, I know. No big deal. I used to call you little darling when we were kids. It's only later that we didn't get along so well. We were too different. And then Richard came along and we went our separate ways. It's been quite a gap. How funny that we've come together again after all this time. When we used to talk on the phone, I hardly recognized your voice. I'm ashamed to admit it.

I'm not the one who moved out.

Yes, of course I know it wasn't you. Let's not start that again. Richard enlisted and I followed him, that's all, there's no more to it than that. Nothing more to be said. But you know, there's an age when you're so focused on yourself that you don't see anyone else.

And now you see me.

Of course. Why else would I worry about you. The hardest thing here is not being black or Arab or Chinese; the hardest thing is to be a woman on her own. Either you become easy prey or you stay home and climb the walls. That's why I slept with that guy, he came on to me in a bar, and now he's chasing after me, but it serves me right. Of course I'm upset about it. I wish he'd just leave me alone.

For a moment, their attention was distracted by some nut running naked in the parking lot—there were all sorts of drugs around, you had no idea what shit people were taking.

If you knew how anxious I was before coming here, Marlene began. I had nothing left. When I say he threw me out, I mean he literally took my things and flung them out the window. I couldn't look at another man, he went crazy with jealousy, there was nothing I could say to him. I went through total hell with him.

I wanted to send a few guys to teach him a lesson but you refused, and I still don't know why. I mean, there are limits. You don't throw a pregnant woman out in the street. You just don't do that. You have to have a smidgen of human dignity.

No, I want to forget about him, that's all. I've already forgotten him. I never want to see him again. This child is never going to know its father's name.

Yeah, that's a good plan. I don't know if it's really possible, but it's a good plan.

Did I tell you he tried to get me locked up. He didn't miss a trick. But I don't want to get my hands dirty. It would mean giving him more importance than he deserves. It was another lifetime.

They had to interrupt their conversation for a pair of Bichons that had rolled in dust and chewing gum. Nath sent Marlene to buy some peanut butter. Alone, she reflected that in less than an hour they'd made up for a good portion of those twenty lost years, and feeling lighter, if a bit doubtful, she began running the spray over the two filthy Bichons.

Finding a good man at a dance was all but impossible. At a gala evening thrown by the army, it was the best they could hope for. Nath had no intention of joining in, but she was curious to watch Marlene do her thing, see how she behaved with men, amid those testosterone-addled soldiers squeezed into their uniforms, who couldn't dance.

It was funny. As a teenager, Marlene had been hot stuff, guys got into her pants pretty easily, and Nath had resented her for that, for the degrading image, but now it was funny to see her so well behaved, sticking to the company of women—cloistered as if in an invisible pen, hair in buns, arms bare, most of them married, hesitant, terrified of life—funny to see her so indifferent to the men surrounding her, so unconcerned by the game of seduction, with so little appetite.

She hoped Marlene would keep giving her such pleasant surprises, that adulthood had finally calmed her down and that finally she'd no longer make Nath ashamed; that Nath would no longer be embarrassed to be seen with her sister, that she could introduce her to friends and sign her up for her yoga class. Two sisters who got along well were a mighty force. Nath discovered how much she had missed it. She almost forgot the discomfort of her high heels, the abominable music, the ghastliness of these straight-laced affairs, all those medals, those absurd buffets, so conventional. She watched her sister until Dan came over to ask for Vincent's address and tell her he was planning to visit him the next day, late afternoon, but first he had to trim that idiot dentist's hedges before the man had an infarction.

The uniform looked good on him. Here was someone who knew how to iron a shirt and crease a pant leg. He, too, looked over at Marlene, who was chatting with the colonel's wife and the wife of his aide-de-camp.

She should find herself someone, don't you think, said Nath. Maybe we should help her find someone.

Don't be silly. I don't want any part of this. Do you see the words dating service written across my forehead.

Never mind. Ask me to dance. Let's not just stand here like dopes. What do you think of her, she asked, resting her hand on Dan's shoulder. She's not bad when she dresses up. I could see her with some upper exec, raising a kid, living a quiet life.

No idea. We're not in her shoes. I mean, you could be right, but it's none of my business.

In any case, the guy shouldn't be too young.

Richard joined them as the song finished. This type of gathering was the last, extremely reduced, mark of respectability that he could lay claim to and he took pride in it, knew how to behave when necessary. It faked out the guys he hung with to see he had entrées with the big shots, and that was all he asked, it was the only medal he cared about.

What say we slip out of here and go get a quiet drink on our own, he said. We've done our bit.

Nath and Dan were all for it. They beat a discreet path toward the door and passed the message to Marlene, who declined the invitation, claiming she was tired and wanted to go home.

You're not tired, Richard told her, just bored silly. And who could blame you.

Saying nothing, Dan went to wait for them outside, where a few gusts of wind were still blowing. The young leaves trembled with a rustle of tissue paper. The sky was clear and stretched impressively far. When you moved away from the lights, the stars came out one by one, the signs of the zodiac reappeared. Marlene was playing a strange game with him. He didn't quite get the rules, but he knew it had begun. No woman could just do things simply.

She never refused to see him, welcomed him into her bed whenever he wanted, and the gentler she acted, the more distant she became. It was weird. She never held anything against him. He would have preferred that she blame him for something. She sometimes fell asleep against his shoulder and when he left, she watched him go without a word and even smiled as he went out the door—that kind of weirdness. But she no longer asked him for anything.

The flags snapped like whips above the barracks. A few strains of music intermittently escaped from the buildings. He removed his tie, stuffed it in his pocket, and unbuttoned his collar. And if he had the misfortune of not seeing her, of being out of touch for two days, she smiled even brighter when he returned, pressed herself against him, caressing and silent, but doubly aloof, so that he pushed her at arm's length to look at her and seek an answer and, with closed face, she slipped between his fingers and busied herself with taking off his jacket.

And now here she was avoiding him and preferring to go home after ignoring him all evening and dancing with every Tom, Dick, and Harry as if he didn't exist. Not that he held it against her. If this was about not displaying their relationship, she was perfect, he couldn't complain. Still, you could take it too far.

Richard thought she was into someone, that she'd spotted some cute blond guy in the crowd and wouldn't be going home alone, he'd bet his bottom dollar on it.

Dan merely emptied his glass while Nath shook her head, deeming that Richard didn't know what he was talking about.

It must be starting to get to her, don't you think, he chuckled. Don't you think so, Dan, and anyway, where's the problem.

If you had asked the same question of every person in that bar—who seemed to be happy as clams there—not one of them would have known where that nagging, exasperating problem could be. The fact remained that

Dan suddenly started asking himself the same thing. The idea that Marlene might be sleeping with someone else hadn't occurred to him. He got up to fetch some more drinks—he downed one at the bar before returning to their table. It was an unpleasant thought. A few drinks were a good idea. Luckily, you had to shout if you wanted to be heard, hence the tendency to stay silent if you had nothing to say. While Richard and Nath started talking to others, he scrunched into his chair and stared at the ceiling.

He buzzed, she answered, he went upstairs, the bedroom door was open, it was two in the morning and she was wearing those flannel pajamas he liked. He'd evidently woken her up. Did I wake you, he asked. She answered with that benevolent, almost tender smile that she reserved for his impromptu visits. He sat down on the bed and she untied his shoelaces.

You seem very strange these days, he said.

No, not really.

Nothing bothering you.

She raised her eyes toward him and shook her head.

So much the better, he said.

He reached out to her and settled her on his knees.

The next morning, armed with a stepladder and a pair of shears that he'd carefully sharpened, he started in on the dentist's hedges, the latter having driven off with his golf clubs. He stretched a rope from end to end to help him cut straight and put on a T-shirt, as it was warm out despite the gusts of wind that furrowed the water in the infinity pool and ruffled the fringes of the taupe-colored umbrellas.

The work wasn't unpleasant and he took a certain satisfaction in it. If his reputation and his integration into the neighborhood benefited, so much the better, an added bonus. After the last storm, he had helped the woman who lived with her backward son up the street to clear her lawn of debris, and since then he'd been getting a few hellos as he returned home from his dawn run. By late morning, he had just finished trimming and was about to clean up when he caught sight of the dentist's wife watching him fixedly from a ground-floor window, naked as a jaybird, hair loose. He pretended not to notice and kept raking up the clippings. Seeing that pallid blonde, with her flat heels and dresses that fell below the knee, her elusive air—it was mind-boggling. He dropped two bags of lawn trash on the curb, and when he came back, she was still there, arms hanging at her sides, as if petrified, chewing her lip, but he didn't dwell on her. Beneath the varnish, the paint was cracking. He hastened to finish his chore and went inside without looking back. The image of that naked woman, whose puritanism and reserve normally chilled his blood, pursued him a moment, under the shower, and even a little later as he vacuumed, dumbfounded by the

almost hallucinatory incongruity of that pale-faced
prude being susceptible to the demons of the flesh. It
was heartening, in its way.

He had no wish to keep debating the matter and he had
nothing to sell. Night was falling; he had been patient.
The request wasn't hard to understand, and it was pointless to let the man jabber on. In the middle of a sentence,
he grabbed him by the hair and banged his head on the
bar. Not hard enough to knock him out, but Vincent
saw stars and wavered on his stool.

You can thank your personal god I'm not her husband,
Dan muttered, sliding the napkin dispenser toward him.
And enough with the dog, too.

Dan swallowed his third shot of Irish whiskey with
honey, an intriguing concoction Vincent had introduced
him to at the beginning of their chat, before things
started dragging on and sounding like a haggle between
rug merchants, with Vincent trying to wheedle some
concessions, the possibility of occasional meetings, like
maybe once every two weeks, or even once a month,
until the moment Dan had slammed his head against the
bar to shut him up.

This is nothing personal, Dan continued. I'm just the
messenger. You seem like a nice enough guy. But as far
as this is concerned, best forget about it and disappear.
I'm saying this for your own good. I'm not the one
who'll come see you next time, and I'm the good cop.

But you don't understand, she's gotten under my skin.
Don't you know how crazy I am about her. I dream
about her every night.

That's too bad. Get it through your head. It would be
too easy. You think you can just waltz in and screw up
twenty years of marriage. Give me a break, not in your
wildest dreams. You're not in the same league, pal,
you've bitten off more than you can chew. You're like
the pauper in love with a princess. I know it's hard, but
you've got to face facts.

I don't think I can handle that.

You're going to have to. Unless you want someone to
break your kneecaps and lord knows what else. Listen
to what I'm telling you. She's not the only one, there are
others out there.

If you can say that, it means you don't understand shit.

Dan signaled to the bartender, who was apparently so
out of it that he hadn't seen Dan bounce Vincent's head
off the counter. How's it going, guys, everything okay,
he asked, yawning behind his pink eyeglasses even
though it was barely eight in the evening.

It means you don't understand how much I hurt, Vincent insisted.

Dan emptied his glass and left without answering.

Nath lost no time finding out what happened. He had no
sooner gotten home and started opening a can of ravioli
than she called.

I'm outside, she said, we can talk freely.

Oh, gosh, I think it all went well, he said. Seems like an okay dude. I relayed your message. But he's got it bad, and I can't guarantee what'll happen next.

So what the hell does he want.

You know perfectly well what he wants.

There was a long silence on the other end.

## SLUT

Over the following days, Dan came to the conclusion that secrecy was no longer viable. It was a huge step—whose consequences he didn't fully gauge—to bring out into the open the relationship he'd been having for some time with Marlene, but they risked hitting a wall if he did nothing.

He couldn't imagine losing her. He couldn't see himself going back to his old life, between solitude, multiform nightmares, bitterness, OCD up the wazoo, and the battery of molecules that kept his head above water. He was doing better since she'd been around, or at least not so bad. And every veteran he knew, without exception, would have killed for the tiniest hint of improvement in their condition, the slightest drop of light that could draw them out of the shadows in their brains.

This leap into the unknown was totally different from parachuting at three thousand feet with an oxygen mask: it was really scary. At dawn, after running for an hour, he sat down in the cool air and the silence and rested his head in his hands to think. And he continued thinking on the rowing machine, or hanging upside down from the bar attached to the doorframe.

During a quick visit to his mother, as a dry run, he mentioned—hesitantly, with many circumlocutions—a woman he'd met and whose company he'd like to keep for a while, but his poor mother was practically gaga now and didn't understand a word he said.

Marlene had long ago realized that she shouldn't rush him. She simply worked it so that he'd fall into her hands like a ripe fruit. She moved forward in small increments, but move forward she did, and every centimeter of terrain conquered was permanent. Sometimes she acted a bit imprudently, stole a furtive kiss between doorways or rubbed against him for an instant when the others weren't looking. If she hadn't been pregnant, if time weren't of the essence, she would have enjoyed staying on that course, which was electrifying and wonderfully whimsical—especially since when the time came, they could sleep together no holds barred.

Despite everything, since Nath had gotten it into her head to marry her off, things had grown more complicated. Officially, she was on the market and couldn't make a face whenever her sister introduced her to someone and Dan got mad every time—even though he knew the game—and preferred to split, turn off his phone, and go home.

One evening when the Toyota dealer organized a cocktail party to launch his new crossover hybrid and Nath and Marlene had gotten dressed to the nines, he bailed, making at least one of them happy.

They were parked more or less in the same spot and the same little old man was walking between the rows, hawking popcorn and fingering his white lock of hair.

You can start taking out your hanky, said Dan, rubbing his hands together after pushing back his seat and reclining.

So, aren't you going to buy me popcorn.

Sure. Of course I will. What made you say that.

She told me so.

He felt his pockets for change.

Skip it, said Mona. I was joking. So this is where you bring them.

Bring who.

Oof, I don't know, the girls you pick up.

No, I generally go to a hotel. Why are you breaking my balls with this. Look around you at all those morons. You think I could screw someone with twelve pairs of eyes gaping at me.

I didn't say anything.

I know. I'm jumping ahead. What else did she tell you. And anyway, what could she say. Ask her about the movie.

142

She undid three buttons of her shirt. It's hot in here, don't you think, she said.

He gazed at her for a second, with a slight apprehension that translated into a vague grimace as he turned his eyes back to the screen.

Laurence Olivier and Greer Garson rock, he declared. Do me a favor and pay attention, will you.

Your green-eyed redhead is in black and white.

Use your imagination.

That might not have been the smartest thing to say.

She wiggled on her seat to pull off her striped leggings.

Sorry, but I'm dying in this heat, she protested.

It was nice out, the evening was mild, but it wasn't as hot as all that.

How far you going to take this.

I have no idea.

What's up. Is it because it's spring.

What do I have to do, beg. Are you doing this on purpose or are you really so clueless. I'm all grown up. I even kiss with tongue.

He turned toward her smiling and asked if she was done. And as she leaned toward him, he gently pushed her away and asked again.

She lapsed into an enraged silence. The thought occurred that the next time he wanted to see a movie, he'd go by himself. She opened the car door and took off at a run. He didn't try to catch her, there would be no point.

She was right not to want to rot here. There was no future for her in a backwater like this, he thought, and it made her nuts like most of the girls her age, and even the others, and even more or less everybody, if you didn't mind generalizations. Nath and Richard had been relieved that she wanted to be a secretary but they were dreaming, they didn't know her, she wanted to become a secretary about as much as she wanted to lop off a leg. She was chomping at the bit while waiting for better days and was ready to try anything—like throwing herself at a guy who was broken beyond repair, who was old enough to be her father and would make her even crazier.

Wallowing in his black mood, he quietly got drunk in his yard, under the moonlight, and ended up slumping onto the grass and spending the night amid the slugs and June bugs.

He didn't hear from Mona for several days, but nothing especially worrisome there. He'd sometimes gotten the silent treatment for a week or more over a simple argument when they were on the same team and he'd flown off the handle at her lousy playing. She could be highly sensitive and it wasn't improving with age. The episode in the car came back to him at regular intervals—with the same intensity as those flashbacks full of blood and dead bodies, except that this one was just sad and dull—and he shook his head, feeling regretful, for things would never again be the same between them.

The minor fights, the minor squabbles and sulks were no more. Clown time was over. They were hurting each other for real now.

He arrived early in the morning when it was his turn to oil the lanes. The bowling alley was closed. He switched on the lights. Compared with the usual hubbub, the reigning silence made the place seem unreal. He hesitated a moment, then rolled a few balls that echoed as if at the rear of a cave. The pins were raised, there was only emptiness at the end of the lane. But he took his time, aimed carefully, applied himself, adjusted his stance, and the ball left his hand, rumbled to the other end, and disappeared without meeting a single target. He remained seated a moment, listening to the silence. Then he put on his overalls, cleaned his hands with sanitizer, and got to work.

Meanwhile, Nath and Marlene arrived at the salon, leaving the door open to air the place out and let in the morning sun that sparkled between the lazy buildings of the shopping center.

Richard had half-awoken on hearing them leave, but he'd been playing cards until dawn and fell back asleep with a grunt while Mona smoked weed at the window of her room and vaguely searched for an excuse to skip her class on Cooperation and Productive Relationships.

The radio announced nice weather until Easter and a few degrees warmer. Dan took advantage of a break to go get two memberships to the pool. He thought of it as a beginning—and not a downward spiral, as the nervous, reptilian, maleficent part of his brain whispered, urging caution. It was still a stiff combat, a cruel dilemma that he expected to get ahead of, to win by forcing his way through it. Running out into the open was sometimes the only means to stay alive.

Nath turned to Marlene and said remind me that guy's name, oh yeah, George, that's right, George, so what didn't you like about him, he's tall, he's not bad-looking, doesn't seem too boring, he's got money, he'll probably get a nice pension. So what is it, the color of his eyes. No, I don't know. Maybe the way he talked to me. It's hard to say.

I see. Seems to me you've gotten awfully choosy.

She trimmed a terrier's whiskers with a snip of the scissors.

Yeah, I was kind of a piece of work, answered Marlene. But that's all behind me now.

For me, it's the opposite. I've come into my own, sexually I mean. With that guy, Vincent, you know, it just hit me. I still can't get over it. I don't have as much experience as you, but even so. You see what I'm driving at.

Oh, listen, that George didn't do it for me, sorry, but I wasn't attracted. He had that awful high-pitched voice. And did you see how he danced. Like a hooked worm.

Richard had won a tidy sum the previous night. He was lost in thought. The offer was tempting. He didn't know

jack about Laundromats, but it seemed pretty simple.
People put coins into machines and in the evening you
came by to gather up the cash. It didn't sound too tiring
and would leave him plenty of spare time. And most of
all, most of all, his income would be regular, in both
senses of the word, and times being what they were,
in this horrible uncertainty, you couldn't afford to be
careless.

When Mona emerged from her room, her father was already gone. Good thing, too, because if she could avoid
talking, so much the better. She'd heard him come in
at dawn and had followed his path by ear from room to
room, a kitchen chair knocked over onto the tile floor,
boards creaking in the hallway, the doorknob that he
turned carefully, the hiss of water in the bathroom sink,
the gurgling of the drain, his return to the bedroom
where the bedsprings made an irritating squeak. She
herself had spent a horrible night. She boiled some water
for tea because smoking made her thirsty, but basically
she didn't feel like anything.

Dan told Richard he'd go check out the launderette with
him in late afternoon, but no earlier because there was
a contest and Brigitte had requisitioned everyone, she
wanted all hands on deck, no exceptions. He was stuck.
But on the face of it, the idea didn't seem too bad. He
took down the address and hung up. Brigitte asked what
he was doing over there. He wasn't being paid to make
personal calls on the clock.

Marlene was eating lunch by herself. She'd gone outside to leave them in peace. She thought Nath was taking a huge risk, but distractions were few and far between and there was nothing worse than losing your desire and succumbing to melancholy. Still, she didn't encourage it. She continued just to see no evil, hear no evil, and that's as far as her role went, especially since her sister didn't ask for more. Anything she could have said Nath already knew. But if you couldn't resist yourself, get a grip on yourself, then who else could. Marlene knew something about this.

She looked at her watch, bit her lip, and cooled her heels on the opposite sidewalk.

Mona had waited a long time for her breasts to start growing. When the miracle had finally occurred—with exasperating slowness—she'd thought Dan would look at her differently, but nothing doing, and since the other evening she'd realized that it would never happen, and she couldn't get over it. She didn't even cry. She was just unable to do anything. She got dressed to go out, but remained sitting in a kitchen chair until daylight started to wane. She hated herself. No kidding, she really couldn't stand herself.

Whatever the case, it was a pleasure to see Richard so excited, so bubbling over with enthusiasm. The machines weren't exactly new and the place needed repainting, not to mention some serious repairs, but he already saw himself as the manager of this palace and in his

hand he held a wad of cash to prove that he was ready
to invest straightaway—it was a mania of his to flash
his money around, and the memory of the night when
they'd cleaned him out hadn't changed a thing.
I have a good feeling about this, he said. I know the
tattoo artist across the street. He says the place is always
packed.
Don't just sign, said Dan. Think it through. But basically, I can see you doing this. It should work for you.
It's like you were dealing with slot machines.
Exactly. It'll be my little casino.
He rested a hand on one of the fat stainless steel washing
machines and stroked its rump while looking around,
eyes shining.
I'm your guy for the paint job, Dan volunteered.
Great. We should go hiking for a day or two. I've got a
few son of a bitch pounds I need to drop.
The minute she got home, Nath jumped under the
shower without running into anyone in the house. She
heaved a sigh of relief. She knew she wouldn't always be
so lucky, but the danger had its good side, brought an
undeniable bonus. Her knees were still shaking.
She started when she saw Mona had come into the bathroom, grimacing and sniffing the air like a bloodhound.
Something stinks in here, she said, lowering her gaze
toward the underwear her mother had tossed in the sink.
Looks like somebody had herself a good time.
Nath stood petrified in the shower stall.

You're disgusting, Mona added, turning on her heels. Nath put on a bathrobe and slowly combed her hair before the mirror. She had just suffered another vicious slap from her daughter.

If Dan had given her an open-ended ticket to travel around the world, with stopovers to die for and super-deluxe hotels, Marlene apparently wouldn't have been happier than when he pulled the two pool memberships from his pocket and handed her one. She took him in her arms and wouldn't let go.

And later, as she was resting her head against his shoulder after having deposited several moist kisses on his belly, she took his hand and squeezed it hard. And the next morning, she took his arm as they walked down the street to go get coffee and he didn't balk.

Dan had seen his shrink after leaving Richard and the man had said it looks like you've found the right woman for you, but he hadn't reacted. The less you told a shrink, even one who was now an old acquaintance, the better. Especially when the latter pressed on a spot where a new pain gently started to hurt, for if Marlene was indeed the right woman for him, his missing half, how could he help thinking that he could also destroy her with all the shit he dragged behind him. How could they manage with that. What kind of life could he offer her, what kind of life would he make her live, what sort of happiness could she expect. He looked at her, all smiles, still under the effect of the night they'd spent together, giving him her arm, blowing on her coffee while holding his hand across the table, and he now found her altogether lovely, and promised himself to do his best—without really knowing what that meant. After spending the day walking through the woods, in the great outdoors, they unrolled their sleeping bags next to a small stream and set about making a fire. They were kneeling. Before, back when they were sent into the combat zone, this trek would have been a piece of cake, carrying gear that weighed a ton, but that was no longer the case; now they surrendered after twelve miles and Richard had blisters.

Darkness was falling, the night looked calm, not too chilly. Richard fried up some cutlets while Dan sliced bread and opened cans of pâté. A rabbit sat watching them for a while and they talked to it, asked after the wife and kids, how things were going in Rabbitland, if he had any pals in the area.

They were in a good mood, content to be together. It brought back some good memories—it hadn't all been bleak—and both of them had at least one good reason to feel happy that evening. They emptied one six-pack of beer and immediately replaced it with another that they fished out of the cold stream.

They were stretched out on their sleeping bags, in socks, feet near the fire, and Richard said that Nath's mood had improved in the last few days and he was sure it was because of his plans for the Laundromat. He was sorry he hadn't thought of it sooner and started laughing at the idea that he'd have to buy a suit and polished shoes.

Dan nodded with a smile. It was like a wilted flower coming back to life in its pot. He'd gotten that expression from Marlene, who'd told him about the resurgence of affection between her and Nath lately. He was happy to be there with Richard. And amazingly, their reunion was the same as with the two sisters, it sprang from the same cause.

And anyway, Nath is right, Richard continued. It'll help me refocus.

I'll let you know when I see a house for sale near me. With those middle-class snobs. Not on your life. When I think about that fucker of a judge, giving me three months. It's not like I killed anyone.

When night fell, they put on insect repellent and moved closer to the fire. They could hear the babbling of the stream, sometimes a croak, the shrill cry of a night bird, the snap of a branch.

But I admit, he resumed, I admit a hint of respectability doesn't hurt. It's pathetic, but that's how it is. I got sick very fast of being a delivery driver, you know that, I wasn't cut out for it. And besides, Nath is happy, she's been very supportive about this. I think it calms her down.

She's right. If they keep lowering our pensions and cutting our retirement benefits, we'll all be out sweeping the streets. With your Laundromat, at least you'll be

able to eat, people will always have dirty clothes. Mona
could help you do the books for a bit of pocket change.
Best not to ask her for anything right now. It's like
talking to a tomb. I have to keep myself from giving her
a smack.

Don't pay any attention. She just needs space.

Yeah. Is that why she stays shut up in her room all day.

I know, but go easy on her.

I am going easy on her. Teens aren't exactly my spe-
cialty. I'm not around enough. I don't know how to talk
to them. I can see how much work it'd have been, if I'd
really gotten into it. A full-time job, and no guarantee
of success.

It's okay, she's doing fine. She's pretty and smart. I
wouldn't worry about her.

I wonder if Marlene is having a bad influence on her. I
wouldn't be surprised.

Dan, who had been staring at the sky, turned toward
him.

What makes you say that.

Oh, I dunno, they see each other a lot. They spend
whole afternoons together, talking. I have no idea what
she's telling her. I have no idea, but she's still a slut.

Dan leaned up on his elbows. That's a good one, he said.

What are you, blind, Richard went on. Marlene is a total
nympho. I fucked her practically as soon as I got out.
No fuss no muss. Just saying, since we're talking about a
bad influence.

Dan lay back down with a grimace, rubbing his stomach.
What's wrong, asked Richard.

I don't know. Maybe something I ate.

He closed his eyes and didn't wake until the next morning. He was covered in dew. Dawn was barely breaking. Over them floated a strong odor of wet ash. Richard was asleep, snuggled in his bag. Dan got undressed and stepped into the stream. He rubbed himself energetically. There was mist, the light was pale and the water really cold, but he needed that at least.

He told Richard he wanted to go back, that he was either going to throw up or have the shits, he wasn't sure which, no doubt the pâté, and they retraced their steps under a clear sky, twelve miles in the other direction; he wanted to run, but supposedly he wasn't feeling well. Richard talked behind him all by himself, or else he was talking to Dan who answered only sporadically and advanced amid the bushes and branches.

Night was falling when they reached the car. Richard asked how he was feeling and Dan made a sign that he felt better. Richard smiled and said that, in that case, he wouldn't mind having a cigarette, especially at dusk, which he especially enjoyed. Dan nodded and leaned against a fender. A few stars were already glinting in the plum-colored sky.

Did you know you were yelling last night, Richard said.

I know. I forgot my pills at the house. I thought I wouldn't need them. Anyway, I'm bushed, I'll drop you

off and go straight home. Hope I didn't get the flu. I'm
sorry.

Forget it. We got a good hike out of it. And don't forget,
we met Johnny Rabbit.

## DEMON

Marlene tried all day to reach him. Her vague annoyance gave way to worry. She had less and less tolerance
for being out of touch with him; she could make do with
messages, phone calls, even a wink, but this time there
was a gap of seventy-two hours, and that was a lot. She
felt sure something was wrong.

That evening, she even prowled around his house. His
car was parked in the driveway but the lights were out.
She tried the bowling alley, where she saw a technician
she knew by sight who told her Dan had called in sick,
he'd come down with the flu.

She stopped at the bar for a drink. At least he was alive.
The lack of communication became all the more mean-
ingful. The next morning, she was so distracted that she
got bitten by a Chihuahua.

Nath wasn't aware of anything, other than Dan had
gone home feeling pretty woozy but that he and Richard
had spent two great days together. Richard was thrilled.
He might have gone to see his mother, Nath added,
coming back from the pharmacy. He visits her two or

three times a year. With the distance, it takes him all day. I'm putting a muzzle on this little shit.

Marlene trapped Dan the next morning at dawn. He was in his yard, bare-armed in an undershirt, raking the leaves though there was scarcely enough light to see and he could have used a jacket.

He remained speechless for a second when he saw her coming.

Then he smiled and made an appeasing gesture while nodding.

But don't come too close, he said. I came down with a bitch of a flu.

Did it paralyze your arm to pick up the phone. Are you bullshitting me, Dan.

I think it's out of juice. I was running a hundred and five for three days, I've only just gotten up. I felt like I was in a tunnel, like I'd dropped acid. You're the first person I've seen since opening my eyes.

It was true that she found him pale, eyes baggy, slightly stooped.

Well, okay, but now that I'm here, let me come in.

No, absolutely not, the doctor's on his way. He knows me. I had a word with him. It might be contagious. It could be some tropical disease I picked up over there, we don't know yet.

She remained silent. She didn't quite know what to make of all this. She felt at once relieved and alarmed. Suddenly, she was no longer angry with him. Daylight

grew to the brightness of a low-watt bulb. She raised
her head.

Well, at least let me kiss you, she said.

No, I can't take that responsibility, no, absolutely not. I
have to follow a protocol, you understand, there are strict
procedures I'm supposed to respect. They're not playing
around with this, and I get it. Please, Marlene, go home,
don't make things harder than they already are.

She hesitated a moment more. She had the instinct of
people who are used to rebuilding from scratch, who try
their best to limit the damage while anticipating what
happens next.

Don't stay out here like this, she sighed, squeezing her
bag under her arm, you'll catch cold.

She grimaced and, turning away, reminded him to
charge his phone.

He didn't move until he'd heard the car door slam
and the engine turn, then fade away with the crowing
of the rooster. Then he raked up the last leaves, his
mind elsewhere. After which it was time for a good
shower. He got undressed, positioned himself under
the shower head, and was reaching for the knob when
he smelled something burning. He immediately pulled
on his underpants and ran out of the bathroom. It was
his sofa starting to catch fire. Under the gaze of Mona,
who was watching the spectacle with arms folded. He
grabbed the extinguisher from the kitchen and put out
the nascent flames, which had nonetheless devoured his

cushions—no telling what they were made of, but they gave off an acrid smoke and out of them jumped glittering sparks and mysterious curlicues.

Once outside, still dazed, he unthinkingly squeezed her in his arms. You're totally out of your mind. You scared the shit out of me.

Howdy, neighbor, called the dentist as he left for work.

Dan let go of Mona, but it was too late.

What the fuck was *she* doing here, Mona said in an ugly voice.

Are you spying on me now.

She's the one you're sleeping with. I can't believe it, she sobbed, falling on him with fists flailing. I can't believe it, you fucking bastard.

He grabbed her arm and dragged her inside before the entire neighborhood was at its windows. He shoved her into an armchair where she remained prostrate, weeping without even realizing it as he got dressed. Then he pulled up a chair and sat facing her. She sniffled.

Call me a cab, she said.

You know, you're going to have learn to deal with this, I think you're going to have to get past it. It's becoming serious. You're wasting your time. You must know that. You must have figured it out by now. There's never going to be anything improper between us. Never ever, and count yourself lucky. This way you'll never have anything to regret. And you can set my house on fire as much as you like, you can roll on the ground and tear your hair out, it's not going to change things.

You're hurting me. Every word you say is hurting me.

Listen, I don't have an answer. You'll have to find it for yourself. Look at this mess. What did it get you.

What do you see in Marlene, can you tell me that.

It's not about her.

You two sure played it close to the vest, I'll say that much. You make me sick, every last one of you. I never want to see you again. Call me a cab, I'll wait outside.

Things had never gone this far, or been this rough. She was hurting him too. He was almost on the verge of tears as he watched her leave. She was like his daughter, and he was feeling it. What Mona had to say, she said straight, without kid gloves. He loved her for that, too, for her rotten nature, her intolerance, but this time it burned like acid. This blow had been totally unexpected. An atomic strike. Everything had flown apart. He spent the morning sawing his sofa in three sections so that he could cram it into the car and bring it to the dump. To the dentist, who was watching, he alluded to a short circuit. You don't happen to play golf, do you, asked the medical man. Dan answered no, struggling to fit a piece of the sofa onto the back seat without ripping the ceiling fabric. In any case, the dentist added as he took his leave, if you don't remember to schedule your cleaning, my friend, it's not my fault. He exchanged a

wave with his wife, who was waiting on the front stoop
to see him off, framed by potted shrubs trimmed into
spirals. At most, you could see her ankles and wrists,
and her hair was in a perfect bun. She met Dan's gaze
for a split second, then immediately looked down.
He scrubbed the living room top to bottom, suddenly
overtaken by a kind of frenzy, on all fours or up on a
ladder to track down the last trace of soot, the smallest
mote of dust, scraping at microscopic stains until he'd
worn down his nails.
Evening found him on the floor, exhausted, sitting
against the wall facing the wide-open windows, through
which came the cool breeze of dusk and its brilliant
colors that made him squint. He raised a hand to shield
his eyes and slowly rolled onto his side. He felt better,
pretty beat but back on the ground, in a clean house,
a living room that shone like a new penny. He could
finally take a shower and pour himself a drink to relieve
the stress of that trying day.
Once again, he was in his underpants when the tele-
phone rang.
Yes, Marlene, I'm fine. I was about to take a shower.
Dan, I've felt rotten all day.
Shit, I hope I didn't give you my germs.
I feel like there's something you're not telling me.
No, I don't have anything of note to report. It's not like
we haven't seen each other in six months.
Is it Richard.

No, why.

I don't know. The kinds of things you men say to each other. Anyway, you know better than I do.

What could he possibly have told me. No, I can't think of anything. I have no secrets from you, Marlene.

Dan, if I lost you, I don't know what I'd do.

I'm not going to die, don't worry. It's not Ebola.

What if I came over and stayed outside. We could talk through the window. I really need to.

But aren't we talking now. Listen, I can't stand in front of a drafty window.

He heard her breathing heavily at the other end of town. It didn't leave him indifferent, but he could take it.

You just have to be patient, he told her.

I can't go home to an empty house. I feel like it's hard to breathe.

Go get a change of scenery. Invite your sister for a walk. Go to the movies, I don't know.

She never has time. As soon as she has a free minute, she's off with her boyfriend.

Wait, are you kidding me. Tell me you're joking.

She's lucky, at least.

He didn't answer. He'd had quite enough of women for one day. He wondered if that's what it meant to be a misogynist. If they needed to gang up in threes to trample him.

Mona committed suicide that night, but they didn't find her until the following evening, at the bottom of the pond, a hundred yards from the old wind pump. Despite her time in the water, they established that she had at least six grams of alcohol in her bloodstream and that half the pills she'd swallowed were not yet absorbed at the time of death, which was ruled by drowning.

Dan awoke with a start, yanked out of one of his habitual nightmares, and what Richard told him was worse than even the grisliest of them. Cold sweat enveloped him. He bounded out of bed in the dark and remained standing, one hand resting on the wall, short of breath, while Richard mumbled some more strangled words that he didn't really hear about the discovery of the body.

Ten minutes later, he arrived at their house, unsteady on his feet. Nath must have taken tranquilizers, as she couldn't get out of her chair, and so he hugged Richard first. The pain was enormous, the shock complete, the horror. He helped Nath stand up and she sobbed into his neck for long minutes—sometimes she stamped her foot on the floor and wailed.

She called Marlene and left a message. Then she went to the window and smoked a cigarette, still weeping silently.

He stepped outside; it was unbearable.

And this was only the start of several nightmarish days until the burial. It began with a weird clash involving Marlene. When she arrived, distraught, Richard laid into her, shouting about the bad influence she'd had on his daughter, and when she asked what he meant by that, he stood mute, then went out slamming the door.

Nath and Dan were dumbstruck. It really wasn't the time for that.

He caught up with her and they walked; he explained that Richard was beside himself with grief, that she shouldn't judge him too harshly. She stopped short, in tears.

And what about you. What's your excuse, she yelled, almost bawling.

Oh, come on, I can't think about all that, I'm in no shape for it, he snapped. I'm devastated.

When her body was laid out, Dan couldn't look at her. He helped Nath pack up her daughter's things in boxes that they stored in the garage. One evening, Richard took part in a race that nearly ended in disaster, so badly did he hurt. He lost several pounds in just a few days. He got drunk two nights in a row, and the morning of the burial he nearly strangled Marlene against Mona's coffin, he completely lost it, and Dan could barely force him back down into his seat. He, too, was torn apart; he too would have liked to strangle someone.

Perhaps himself, for starters. Or else plant a knife in his heart for the part he'd played in this tragedy. To think about it was dreadful. His own life wasn't worth much, and anyway he no longer expected anything from it, but it was Mona's that had been taken, and that was intolerable. Sometimes he had to sit down, it didn't matter where he was, and he cradled his head in his hands, moaning.

Marlene was wrong to hover around him right now, he couldn't take care of her, he didn't really see her, he didn't need to feel her nearby. Especially given that business with Richard, who'd got it into his head that Marlene was evil, so to make matters worse there was no way for them to be in the same space. Teetering on the edge of a precipice must have felt like this. A mix of affliction and madness.

He could barely eat anything, nothing would go down, and his morning exercises suffered for it. Despite what Marlene said, what he needed wasn't a good thick steak. He even tried kneeling in church and waiting, but not much came of it.

The little energy left to him he devoted to Richard, who split his time between picking fights, brooding, and tallying the day's earnings before rolling up the coins in a deathly silence.

Dan gave him as much time as possible, as the episode at the burial had been worrisome, his explosion of fury against Marlene staggering; Richard could get out of control, go crazy. He knew what that was like. He'd seen it in action.

But what do *you* think about it, Marlene asked him as he was buying flowers for Mona.

Pestered by a bee, he grimaced. Listen, he answered, I haven't had time to wonder about it.

You think I've slept with half the town, is that it. You believe everything he tells you, am I right.

I can't talk about that now, Marlene. I'm sorry, it's not penetrating my brain. It's all muddled up, all of that got swept away, I'm sorry. I really loved her and I can't get over this. I haven't even been able to tell my mother what happened.

Now that they were kissing only on the cheek, she stood stiff as a pike when he leaned toward her to say good-bye. She remained there an instant without moving as he turned away. She measured the distance they'd fallen just as they were reaching the summit. They'd been struck by lightning and had tumbled even below base camp.

Nath hadn't been back to work in several days and Marlene was overwhelmed. When Vincent burst into the salon, she was on tiptoes, busily inspecting the ears of a Doberman that was standing on the grooming table. She didn't wait for him to open his mouth, but announced that Nath had just lost her daughter in an accident, which no doubt answered most of his questions. He flinched at the news.

Can I do anything to help, he finally asked.

No, I don't think so. My advice is to stay away. Her husband is kind of a psychopath, and I'm not just saying that. Yemen, Afghanistan, Iraq, the whole nine yards.

Yeah, well, I'm a black belt in judo.

That's better than nothing, I guess—you don't get hurt as badly when you fall.

Evenings, she dined alone. She ate what was lying around or ordered a pizza that lasted her two days. She ate by herself because Dan flatly refused to leave Richard and Nath alone together, judging that they'd never make it. He didn't wonder how Marlene was going to make it, and she came to the conclusion that either he just didn't care enough about her or he was really stupid. Possibly both.

Generally, the second day's pizza went straight into the trash and she ate an expired yogurt with stale muesli. Dan thought the same thing. That he'd rather be alone and that he'd been stupid. The failure of his attempt with Marlene was a reminder that he'd been wrong to deviate from his path, chase after a mirage. But the mirage wouldn't go away. Not a day went by when she didn't give him some kind of reminder. She didn't exert much pressure, either—which in itself could prove worrisome, for different reasons—but she was there, somewhere in his frame of reference, never very far.

He wasn't lying when he told her he hadn't been thinking about the problem. Whenever he tried to focus on it, his brain crashed, spun on empty, and it took him a moment before he could recover and go about his business, stricken by a passing dizzy spell.

What's with you, why are you always defending her, Richard grumbled, holding the ladder while he changed the last bulbs in the ceiling.

I'm not defending her. I merely said that if you're talking about bad influences, Marlene isn't the only one around. Don't dump it all on her.

It's just something I feel. I can't explain. You could just trust me once in a while, you know. If I say it's something I feel, it's something I feel.

All done. You can turn them on.

Often it's all in the lighting. Dan had given the place a once-over with the paint roller the night before while Richard shifted and rewired the machines. Two plastic rubber plants decorated the entrance; a few strings of lights, a water fountain, and new cushions for the seats completed the scene. They had worked hard.

I added a dimmer for the spotlights. So what do you think.

Richard nodded vaguely.

You always end up paying for what you do, he said. Sooner or later.

Dan was washing his hands. If only that was true, he answered, rubbing harder.

The one respite he found was with Ralph, who was good-hearted enough to tell him reassuring and comforting things when it was all falling apart, when the shock waves were keeping them all prisoners.

Fact is, Ralph concluded, if I had any advice for Marlene, I'd tell her to pack her bags and go back where she came from. It would be for the best. Richard would end up calming down. I know he's been spoiling for trouble almost every night. It's understandable. He probably doesn't know how else to get it out of his system. Anyhow, if I were her, I wouldn't go near a wounded animal.

Yeah, but she's not going to leave. I'd be surprised. She's not even thinking about it, she's standing firm, saying she's got nothing to blame herself for. And the thing is, I kind of believe her. Richard's got it wrong.

Whether she's lying or telling the truth, sighed Ralph, doesn't change a thing. Richard's not the kind of guy you can reason with. A real hothead, and you know it.

Ralph wheeled his chair outside and showed the new loops his drone could do, making it flutter in the clear sky with a blissful smile on his face.

Dan had the evening off, Nath and Richard having gone to the veterans' raffle that pulled in half the town. Maybe his first moment of peace. He settled to one side of the house so as not to be visible should Marlene venture into the sector. And as night fell, he sat with his glass, watching the stars appear in the sky minute by minute, thinking of his final conversation with Mona, the awful row they'd had. It seemed so unfair. There should be a Trash function, like on a computer.

He was riffling through his memories, bypassing his glass and drinking Three Rivers rum straight from the bottle, when the dentist appeared on his stoop.

A bit chilly to be lounging on the lawn, isn't it, the neighbor called out. But I imagine you've known worse. Surviving in extreme conditions. You veterans are really something, let me tell you. So, you're not going to the raffle.

No, I've got the flu. Enjoy yourself.

Nothing serious, I hope.

Nope, I've known worse.

Alone again, he closed his eyes. He'd been weak enough to think that his return to civilian life could never be as hard as the hell he'd been through, but that only showed how naive he'd been. Had he found peace, forgetfulness, fulfillment. Had he even found rest, some decent sleep. Had he known boredom, the soothing and delicious boredom of a day that was banal, dreary, transparent, ordinary. No, obviously not, nothing of the kind. The journey aboard the ghost train never ended.

He was considering extending his communion with the Three Rivers—although the alcohol was already fogging up his mind—when he sensed he was being watched.

The night was silent and black, you couldn't have seen a thing if not for the laborious clarity of an April moon that was in its last phase before total darkness. He stood up, examined his surroundings, and ended up noticing her. He leaned forward and looked again.

She was standing facing him in the patio doorway, motionless, half concealed by sparse Thujas and again stark naked, pale as a candle, arms hanging, hair fallen to her shoulders. Not very sexy out of context, but put in perspective, she was dynamite.

He got up without giving himself time to think. Nor, in truth, were his thoughts very clear. Screwing this woman went against every rule of good-neighborliness that he'd set for himself and it filled him with an unwholesome joy, like Mr. Hyde, thrilling to put in peril, before even laying a hand on her, everything he'd so patiently built up in hopes of joining the club.

Strange woman. She barely said a word in all the time they were together. She probably had nothing to say, and so much the better. She grunted, hissed between her teeth, cried out when he penetrated her, let out a smattering of obscenities, but nothing that qualified as an actual conversation. Still, she didn't remain passive, and he was surprised by her initiative, as he had imagined her stuck up, blushing at the drop of a hat. She bit, scratched, but within reasonable limits, unless in the heat of action he no longer felt pain. Or else she squeezed him in her arms like a woman possessed and knotted her legs around his loins and he didn't know how to disengage himself other than putting a hand over her mouth as if he'd heard a noise. But there was one thing about which she seemed especially crazy, famished, to the point where it became touching, and that was French kissing. She didn't want to let his mouth go, she remained glued to it, and that was the most astonishing part of all, to imagine that woman naked on top of him, a real sorceress, whereas she was thinking only of a long, ardent kiss.

When they'd finished, he went back to his deck chair. Theoretically, he should have rushed to the shower, but he wanted to enjoy a bit more of that calm he needed so badly. The evening had grown cooler. He imagined the dentist with his raffle tickets. He leaned forward slightly to see if she was still there, but she had gone. It didn't matter, he knew he hadn't dreamed it. He'd just had his neighbor's wife on the bathroom floor and that was the last thing he needed. Mona's grave was still fresh, everything was falling to pieces, everyone was going nuts, and he could find nothing better to do. He snorted sadly. Tears still came to his eyes, without warning, without him even feeling them; people sometimes told him, Dan, did you know you're crying, and he was the most surprised of all.

The pink moon had paled. He wiped his eyes. He saw that Marlene had sent him a text, but he didn't answer. Needless to say, she wanted to know where he was, what he was up to, it didn't vary much. He was lucky she had a job and her freedom was limited by her work hours, otherwise he wouldn't have been able to budge without running into her.

The next day, as he was brushing his teeth, he spotted her on the stoop, waving to her husband. She was perfectly coiffed, ready to go, all prim and proper, distant, as she had always appeared to him—an illustration of the modern woman from out of a 1950s home journal, with her long immaculate skirts, no doubt starched, her buttoned blouses tight at the wrists, her flat shoes, her pearl necklace. They were predicting a bit of rain that day, but that didn't prevent him from mounting his bike and speeding to the bowling alley before impure thoughts got the better of him. He didn't even bother making his bed, something that hadn't happened in years.

At opening time, Marlene was pleasantly surprised to see Nath arriving, not looking very well but ready to get back to work. Marlene hugged her close and murmured some loving words in her ear. The poor woman was just a shadow of her former self, she had aged ten years in a week, lips gray, eyes dull, and the rain that started to fall, darkening the low sky, only made it worse.

Nath didn't know if she could get through this, and it wasn't looking hopeful. She began by sitting down, shattered. She repeated that she didn't for a second share Richard's obsession about the bad influence her sister had had on Mona, but nothing could change his mind, he flew into a rage as soon as she put his word—his abominable accusation—in doubt; and she lived with him, he was all she had, she loved him and tried to avoid contradicting him so as not to aggravate the situation.

Marlene reassured her, it wasn't what Richard
thought that counted, she didn't give a hoot what he
thought, he had always been distant with her, even
acrimonious—and if there was one thing she really
regretted, she added to herself, it was having slept with
him. No, only Nath's opinion mattered, the belief she
had in her sister's innocence, which Dan also shared.
She bit her lip. And speaking of Dan, she continued,
listen, there's something I have to tell you.
So no more cover-ups, shadows, silences, no more of
their oppressive, murderous secrecy. Gripped by an
uncontrollable need, she was about to take a step into
the void, spill everything, she couldn't take it anymore.
She was going to expose their relationship to the light,
come what may.
She took her sister's hand and a deep breath. Squalls
of rain were whipping against the windows, thunder
rumbling in the distance, when the door burst open and
Vincent sprang in like a demon out of a box.
In the time it took them to react, he yanked Nath from
her chair and, without a word, coldly determined, hus-
tled her off under his arm and stomped back out, heed-
less of her complaints, her feeble kicks.
Nath reappeared a minute later, glowering, soaked to
the skin.
Jesus, I thought he'd kidnapped you, Marlene cried,
dropping her raincoat.

He did kidnap me, what do you think it was. It just didn't last long, that's all. I asked him who the hell he thought he was, and if he wanted me to rip his eyes out. He saw I meant it.

Marlene brought her some towels. Nath had sat back down and begun crying in silence.

My poor baby, said Marlene, stroking her head. Look, this isn't really the time, I know, but it's about Dan. And me.

Nath slowly raised a damp, dark eye toward her.

Oh, please, she scowled, give me a break. Stop dreaming. You'd be better off thinking about something else. You're due in six months. So cut it out. Please. I've heard enough for one day.

## INTRUSION

Despite her grief, she was not entirely deaf, or unable to think. She pondered Marlene's words about Dan and they bore their little channel through her mind. She watched her sister all afternoon and the exercise provoked short circuits, sparks in her skull. The rain wouldn't let up. Fat droplets struck the steaming asphalt like shrapnel, blue oblong clouds skidded above the rooftops almost as fast as jet trails, and the wind was in especially good form.

As she was locking up the salon, she suddenly realized that she loathed her sister. She couldn't believe it. She froze under the shock, key still in the door. And as Marlene, behind her, asked if there was a problem, she slowly turned and gave her a furtive, distrustful look, full of resentment, that her sister didn't notice, absorbed as she was in her own thoughts and still smarting from Nath's unexpected rebuff a few hours earlier, which seemed to wipe out all her hopes. It was getting dark. The rain had ended but it was as if the wind were out looking for it.

Richard was leaning with a lamp over the engine of his Alfa when she arrived. He looked up and followed her with his gaze until she had disappeared inside. She set her bag on the kitchen table and, unable to take another step, collapsed into a chair without bothering to remove her parka. She stared awhile into the emptiness, floored by the revelation that had suddenly come to her—but which wasn't so incredible if you thought about it. It wasn't that she'd suddenly started agreeing with Richard, who wouldn't let go of his vain accusations—that wasn't the problem. The problem came from an old well of bitterness that had risen to the surface and been gushing like blood from an open wound ever since Marlene had mentioned her interest in Dan. It came from everything this meant to Nath, everything it stirred in her that had remained buried in the depths of her being.

There was no food in the house. As so often lately. Anyway, they had lost their appetites, didn't even think about eating. Richard, who was six feet tall and weighed two hundred pounds, could subsist on a biscuit, half of which he'd leave somewhere. Still, she willed herself out of her seat and checked through the cupboards. When you stood in the kitchen, you had to avoid looking toward the hallway so as not to see the door to Mona's bedroom. Which they had locked by mutual agreement, without any marker or sign. She found a few eggs, some bread in cellophane. Through the window, she saw Richard with his headlamp who wasn't bothered by the falling dark and remained absorbed in the engine of his Alfa. She thought about that bitch, that cunt Marlene, while cutting an apple into slices. She lit the oven. She felt as if she was regaining part of her lost vitality. She might have gone through rough patches with her daughter, but she was discovering just how much she had loved her, just how much Mona's death was destroying her. She defrosted a pie crust, after extricating it with difficulty from the block of ice in which it was embedded. She knocked on the window and signaled to Richard that it would be ready in ten minutes. Honestly, it took a hell of a nerve to show up as she'd done, with all her luggage in tow. After eighteen years. Despite what she'd thought, Marlene hadn't settled with age. She had only gotten worse. She'd just learned to conceal it better. She changed out of her work clothes, pulled on a pair of sweatpants, and went back to the kitchen to hunt down some wine. She noticed she had a whopper of a bruise on her thigh, no doubt from when Vincent had shoved her into the front seat and she'd banged against the stick shift, and she tried to think up an excuse. She basted the crust with egg yolk, sprinkled sugar on the apples, and put the pie in. It wasn't exactly fine cuisine, but it was the thought that counted. She decided that she'd see, improvise when the time came. She gestured to Richard that his drink was waiting for him. She heard the wind howl behind the front door. After letting her get out, Vincent had sped off in the middle of the downpour. It was dangerous in his condition. He hadn't realized that Mona's death signaled the end. As if it were so hard to understand. It was Marlene that Vincent should have carried off, once and for all. From the start, Richard had been up front about his antipathy toward her sister. He was blinded by his conviction that Marlene had led their daughter astray, but the fact was, his instincts had warned him Marlene was toxic and her rage against her sister doubled. He was the one who'd seen clearly.

She needed to come back to him, put an end to her straying, which she now saw as a major leak that threatened to sink their old vessel. Especially since her feelings for Richard, so often manhandled by both of them, persisted come hell or high water. She looked at him again, as he looked at the Alfa with hands on his hips, satisfaction on his face, and for the first time in ages she felt a wave of tenderness for the man rush through her.

An aroma of baking apples filled the air.

Later, about to fall asleep, she nestled against him.

That was good, he said.

Next time I'll make it with applesauce, she said in a sleepy voice.

I didn't mean *that*, he replied.

It was late, but Marlene was still pacing around her studio, and the walls were starting to close in. She couldn't understand what was going on with Nath, still less what she might have done to earn such a reaction. She felt lost and disillusioned, yet again. Her life was just an uninterrupted series of disappointments and half-assed adventures, so she shouldn't be surprised by anything. Except that she'd believed in Dan. With alarming naïveté, no doubt, and her abominable tendency to take wishes for realities, but she'd believed. She was the right woman for him, the one he needed, even if he didn't know it yet. True, their relationship was no longer going so smoothly since Mona's suicide had blown it all to smithereens, but she had hung on—she was hanging on, anxious that the redemption she'd no longer dared hope for was slipping through her fingers, and that evening the building was pitching and tossing worse than ever. She was cursed. She knew she could be a better mother, a more perfect wife than any woman she knew, but it was she who would again be watching the parade pass by.

She felt up to telling Dan she was pregnant. That kind
of accident happened more often than people imagined,
and she thought of Dan as the type of man who could
accept it, rise to the occasion, not get caught up in the
usual, alienating platitudes that only appealed to the feeble of mind, the faint of heart, and their wretched brats.
She stretched out fully dressed on her bed. Starting over
was a delusion. Giving up on it was the mark of great
wisdom or total numbness. But she was neither wise nor
prepared to stay in bed waiting for the end of days. She
got up.

It wasn't very easy to get into Dan's place without rousing his attention. He was trained to detect the slightest
sound, sleep with one eye open, and that faculty, which
made him such a valued member of his unit, had saved
his and his buddies' lives more than once. Someone was
in the garden—he sensed it before hearing a sound.
Ever since Mona had set his couch on fire, he'd sat on
the floor, leaning against the wall and using an adjust-
able tray to protect his genitals from the harmful rays
of his laptop. He used to enjoy lying on his couch in the
dark with just the light from the screen. It was full of
memories, that couch, and despite what he claimed, he
missed it. So now he just sat on the floor, and had only
to shut his computer quickly to plunge the room into
total darkness. Someone was creeping near the wall. His
reflexes immediately returned. He stood up without a
sound. He was barefoot, but he didn't have time to put

on shoes. He slipped outside, quieter than an Angora cat, and skirted around the house to take his visitor from behind. He flattened into the corner, ready to trip the intruder and leap onto him, ready to break his neck, but it was Marlene, goddammit, he cried out, goddammit, Marlene, what the hell are you doing here, I could have killed you.

Surprised, she'd jumped back. Oh my god. Oh you scared the life out of me, she said, hand to her chest. I hope I'm not disturbing you. Were you sleeping.

No, I wasn't sleeping. What's going on.

Nothing, nothing's going on. I wanted to see you. No, strike that, I *needed* to see you. Hey, it's not exactly balmy out here, can we go inside.

He didn't answer and headed in.

He switched on a lamp. She said oh, what happened to your couch.

Here, take the armchair, I'll sit on this one.

Yeah. Okay. It looks a little like a temp office in here, don't you think. Could we have a drink, maybe light a few candles.

No, no candles, there's nothing to celebrate. I'm into rum at the moment.

He headed to the kitchen, turned on the light, took a few steps toward the fridge and noticed that the floor tiles were sticky under his feet. He halted, felt his chest contract, his heart race, lowered his eyes, and discovered it was blood. He grimaced, turned around slowly to look behind him and found himself at the end of a large stream of blood that ran from the hem of his pants to the doorway over the cream-white tiles. A river of blood.

He gritted his teeth to keep from screaming.

Marlene called to him, and as he didn't come, she joined him in the kitchen and found him squatting, huddled in a corner near the fridge, eyes wide as saucers and trembling like a leaf. There was a little blood on the floor, some minor smears leading to him.

She rushed forward. He was shaking, hyperventilating.

Dan. Okay, breathe, she said.

She leaned toward him and managed to have a seizure of her own. She collapsed, sprawled at his feet, like a limp rag. He remained unresponsive, huffing like a forge, unable to come to her aid, to make the slightest movement toward her. The wind moaning outside mixed with the hiss of air pushed out by his lungs.

She opened her eyes a few minutes later while Dan, in his corner, was just finishing counting backward by threes from five hundred.

Everything's fine, she stammered, raising herself on one elbow, dazed, not knowing what she was saying.

He nodded slowly, his breathing still hesitant, white as a sheet, forehead clammy, arms folded over his chest where his palpitations were taking their sweet time to calm down.

She reached out a hand to touch him, gave him the pale smile that a loving mother gives her sick child, and stood up unsteadily, tugging on her skirt that had hiked to her waist.

Stay right there, I'll take care of everything, she said while he closed his eyes.

She ran him a warm bath. Inspecting his medicine cabinet, she found bandages, compresses, antiseptic, and some remaining bubble bath scented like candy that she sprinkled into the tub before returning to his side to play nurse.

He emerged little by little. She glanced at his wound, which wasn't very serious, and which she cleaned delicately as he watched with a kind of infantile gratitude. We really make quite a pair, the two of us, she joked while ripping open the bandage wrapper. The cut was hardly bleeding anymore.

He still felt weak, nauseated, strung out. She helped him up and he let himself be led hobbling to the bathroom. He recoiled when he discovered the candy scent that immediately reminded him of Mona, but she was already starting to undress him, unbutton his shirt, and seeing that he wasn't moving, that he remained frozen like a vegetable in a rest home, she made him sit on the edge of the tub to take off his pants and his underwear in the same motion. She smiled vaguely when her eyes fell on his tiny willy shriveled by the brutal events, but didn't let herself dwell on it.

Still in a stupor, he hadn't yet uttered a single word, apart from grunts that might have been words, but when he sank into the hot water—often touted, and rightly so, as mankind's finest achievement—when he lowered his entire body into it with crass enjoyment and a sigh that could have split an oak, he turned to Marlene, kneeling next to him on the electric blue nonskid bath mat, stretched out a hand on which small lemony-scented clumps of foam quivered like whipped egg whites, and said holy fuck, Marlene, we really caught it that time. I think maybe you should fix us some drinks. Mine's rum, like I said. Make it a double.

Before he could move, she stole a quick kiss on his cheek and jumped to her feet. She looked so happy it was a pleasure to behold. He heard her busying herself in the kitchen—she was quite capable of breaking a few glasses—and snorted. She was something else, that woman, he had to admit, keeping his foot out of the water. A kind of half-salty, half-sweet cocktail with just a spritz of seltzer and two or three dashes of angostura. He was impressed by how she'd handled the situation, her effectiveness when she wasn't falling faint herself. She returned to her spot and they clinked glasses. It was good, but it was better still when she began massaging his neck and shoulders.

Oh Jesus God, he blurted in a hoarse voice. Whatever you do, don't stop. I swear, you must have been a geisha in a former life.

She did nonetheless stop to go fix them another round. It had been some time since they'd felt this close, he mused. His run-in with the crazy woman next door had left a taste of putty in his mouth, and that might have explained part of it.

She came back with the glasses and a radio softly diffusing background music for insomniacs, who would listen to anything.

It's a shame we can't light some candles, she said. It would do you good, they're so relaxing.

With eyes closed, he nodded for a few seconds. Oh, all things considered, maybe you're right, he sighed. This could get ridiculous. Do what you like, you're right, you'll find everything in the third left-hand drawer in the sideboard. Bring some candlesticks too, so they don't drip all over the place.

She went out on a cloud. He remained pensive. Since Richard had thrown cold water on him by declaring Marlene a whore and that he'd fucked her himself, Dan had slowed things way down with her—not cut ties, exactly, but the revelation had cooled him, even though in his heart of hearts he fought against being so narrow-minded, so conventional, so morally predictable, but the result was the same. Embarrassed, he playfully fingered the iridescent foam, admitting a bit late in the day that he was in no position to judge, given all the blood he had on his hands.

I took the opportunity to wash the kitchen floor, she announced on her return.

It was nice of you to think of it, he said.

He watched her with growing interest as she carefully arranged the candles in strategic spots. He noticed he was looking at her differently. She lit them, then turned off the overheads. She seemed delighted.

We should put in a little more hot water, he said. It's getting lukewarm.

Now shadows were dancing on the walls, which had turned the color of honey; you'd have to be cross-eyed not to see that she had turned that cold, ugly bathroom into a marvelous grotto, a bit sappy, perhaps, but given the late hour, it fit. He lifted his hands from the water to applaud. She leaned over him to turn the faucets, and as she did so he reached for her breasts and cupped them out of her bra. She regulated the temperature and stood up. She emptied her glass as he watched her, smiling, then performed a striptease for him. They were playing music well suited to this type of dance and she acquitted herself admirably. The candles really were a good idea. On her body, which she revealed little by little, the light made fantastic effects. He loved that little belly of hers, her firm thighs, her breasts, especially her breasts, the texture of her skin. He had sat up, hands crossed behind his head, and he had the urge to smoke a cigarette. Her pink panties made him feel drunk. And when she stripped them off, he groped for his lighter. And when she climbed into the bathtub with him, he exhaled a long puff of smoke at the ceiling.

Later, when they were lying on the bed, he told her she was the only woman to ever share his bedroom.

Get out of town, she said.

No, really, I've always done it somewhere else. Maybe one time, when I was a teenager, but it was my parents' room, not mine, so I don't think it counts. She curled against him.

And so what does that mean, she asked.

I dunno. Maybe it doesn't mean anything. Mona knocked some sense into all of us.

It's funny how there's always something mysterious in what you say.

No. Nothing mysterious at all. It doesn't mean anything more than it says. If you ask me if I like being here with you, I'll say yes and it doesn't mean any more than that. I don't know. Maybe we're compatible, maybe we're not.

He heard the dentist coming home. It must have been two in the morning; the night was black and the wind had more or less died down.

What do you want to know about me, she murmured in his ear. My life is a long story, and not a very pretty one. Do you want to know if I've slept with guys. I'm about to turn forty, I'm not married, of course I've slept with guys. What about you.

I didn't ask.

She almost added and you know what can happen when you sleep with guys who are careless, you get pregnant, but she chickened out, not wanting to jeopardize the ground they'd gained. She had come on a whim, aware how little he appreciated unexpected visits, and had dreaded the worst. But suddenly fate had turned in her favor. Proof that you should never give up on forcing a situation.

She rolled onto her stomach and offered him her behind, thinking that her intrusion, her audacity, had already been hugely rewarded.

## SNAG

Dan, I just want to warn you, Nath said one morning. I'm saying this for your own good. She's my sister, I know her.

He turned toward her, squinting; it was a bright, beautiful day.

Listen, he said, I don't really feel like talking about this. I'll have my coffee and be off. Richard's waiting.

But you don't understand, it's not right, you can't do this. Are you insane. Marlene. You've got to be out of your mind. When Richard finds out. No, really, Dan, I'm stunned. It's a sick joke.

He took a step back and looked at her with an inquisitive smile.

Oh, for God's sake, I'm dating your sister, stop making such a big deal of it. It's not like I asked her to marry me, take it easy, what's gotten into you.

Dan, before she came here, we were a family, and she's going to destroy what's left of it, that's what's gotten into me.

She's not going to destroy anything, he said, setting down his cup. Anyway, I should get moving.

So what this is doing to me, what it will do to Richard— you don't really care, do you.

And what is it doing to you.

I'm not joking. She'll rip you to shreds.

A gloomy prediction, but there wasn't much danger of that, as he already considered himself in shreds. On the other hand, the news wasn't exactly being embraced and it boded ill for the future if she and Richard stuck to their guns. Neither of them had ever felt the need, much less had the time, to voice an opinion about the women he slept with—no more than he, moreover, who regularly forgot to jot down their phone numbers; the idea of a moderately lasting relationship was alien to him, given his physical exhaustion and the narrow space he could have allotted them.

The difference with Marlene was probably that she had come at just the right moment, after his years of trying had yielded such paltry results, and he was getting older, and Mona had nuked everything, and Marlene seemed to need him as much as he needed her. Call it favorable conditions, a fortuitous alignment of the planets—it was the only way he could explain it.

He stopped at the Laundromat to wait for Richard, who was supervising the return of a dryer that he was calling pure junk to a manufacturer's technician who couldn't have cared less—you could tell he was a pro, the type who'd long ago decided not to give himself an ulcer. Fuck me, those Swiss machines are pieces of shit, Richard grumbled, getting into the car. Lifetime guarantee, my ass.

He calmed down as they drove through town, and he raised his shirt collar and put on the tie Dan had brought him—managing a Windsor knot in two shakes—but he wasn't relaxed enough to hear what Dan hoped to tell him about his idyll with Marlene.

They arrived at the military cemetery. Two commandos had been blown up by a mine and that morning they were being given last honors; a few women broke down sobbing, men clenched their jaws, and those who were doing neither wore shades against the glare. Dan and Richard stood with veterans who were all thinking the same thing. Thank you God for not choosing me. Thank you God for letting me come home, even if it isn't as great as I thought it would be. Thank you God for letting me be here, alive, despite all the shit I've gone through.

It was nice out. The service was long but appropriately so, as you couldn't bury these boys in just five minutes. The few children present started to get fidgety, some birds cheeped in the trees in the background, bees gathered pollen from the flowers on the graves, otherwise no one in the rows made a sound.

The civilian cemetery was adjacent. Richard swiped a handsome bouquet on his way in, so as not to show up empty-handed.

One of them had a really pretty wife, said Richard, did you notice.

The brunette in high heels with pale skin and bangs.

Yeah, a shame.

They followed an alley of cypresses and emerged into the newest section of the cemetery, where no trees were growing yet, not a tuft of grass, no tombstones, everything provisional, barely trimmed hedges still in their pots, crosses you could rent by the month. Before the mound of earth that covered Mona, Richard squatted to change the flowers and arrange the new bouquet.

So, go figure, I've been seeing Marlene, Dan blurted out. Who'd a thunk it, eh.

Richard slowly raised his head and turned toward him. Then he stood up, dusted off the knees of his pants for no reason, and asked him to repeat what he wasn't sure he'd heard right.

I know what you're thinking, answered Dan. But you're wrong. Let's not argue about it. I didn't make the decision lightly.

Richard glowered at him steadily. Dan realized there was a good chance they'd come to blows.

It's either her or me, Richard finally stated. Your choice. You decide.

Don't make me do that. Don't make me do something I'll regret for the rest of my life. No matter which way it goes.

You'll come crawling back with your tail between your legs, but by then it'll be too late. I won't even acknowledge you in the street. You'll be dead to me.

Dan shoved his hands in his pockets and looked away. Richard, an evil look on his face, took advantage to spring on him, but so awkwardly that their collision resulted in a brutal and depressing embrace, leaving them momentarily confused, embarrassed, not sure what to do next, nor how to process what had just happened.

Then they pulled apart without a word, and Richard turned his back on Dan to deal with the flowers.

You see the shit she stirs up, he said between gritted teeth. Doesn't that tell you enough. Can you really be that blind.

He glanced behind his shoulder to gauge Dan's reaction, but the latter was already moving away, meditating amid the unmarked plots, the pending graves.

This was off to a bad start. He found a semblance of peace and quiet at the bowling alley, where he kept to himself. That evening, coming home, he was disconcerted for a second when he found her in the house, cooking dinner, but then he remembered he'd given her

a key. Hey, he went in a lighthearted tone. But his heart
wasn't very light after what had happened with Richard,
and earlier with Nath; it wasn't easy to swallow.

You look worried, she said.

No, I'm okay. I just don't like burials.

Aren't you getting changed.

Yeah, sure. You know, this isn't going to be easy, with
those two. They really don't want to see us together.

They don't have to. We can make our own friends.

We'll go to different bars. I'll visit them once in a while.

Even that, I wouldn't recommend.

He took off his leather jacket and went to hang it up, but
couldn't find the coat-rack. Marlene, he called from the
foyer, wasn't there a coat-rack here, with a duck's head.

Oh, yeah, I broke it, I'll tell you about it, it's too
ridiculous.

No problem. If you put it somewhere, I'll repair it.

I threw it out. It was kaput.

You know, that was a present I made for my dad when I
was ten. I spent my entire allowance on it.

Oh, please don't tell me that.

It's okay, I guess I wasn't really all that attached to it.

Oh, uh, while we're on the subject, I broke a vase.

Fine. Did you vacuum. Because, you know, I walk
around barefoot.

He draped his jacket over the back of a chair.

That smells good, but don't make too much. I'm feeling
a bit queasy tonight.

We just won't worry about them, that's all. We don't owe them any explanations.

No, but they were my only family, I don't have anyone else. I don't know where I'd be if it hadn't been for them. I wasn't in very good shape when I got back.

She spun around quickly to turn off what she had on the stove.

Listen, she said, let's just go see them. We're not bad people, we're not criminals, we should be able to talk to one another.

I'm not so sure.

If you don't want to, I'll go alone.

Meanwhile, Richard had gone to bed, without eating and in a foul temper. Nath had made him recount the scene in minute detail and he felt the weight that had settled on his shoulders. Dan had knocked him senseless; he felt utterly betrayed. That bitch. Just from fucking her he had sensed something funny, sensed Marlene was bad karma, and he didn't need that. They should never have agreed to take her in, welcome her, he would have vetoed it if he hadn't been so dumb. But he'd let himself be bought and it was the eternal backlash.

He'd turned off the light. By the faint glow of his alarm clock, he made out Nath's outline coming into the room and sitting on his side of the bed. He didn't need to see her to guess her mood. He had left her in front of her extra-wide TV screen holding a glass of wine and she was like an ice statue sculpted with a chisel. What had happened in the cemetery, in front of their daughter's grave, what he and Dan had said to each other, had left her exasperated.

No point in talking to her when she was like this.

Normally, he would have gone out and tried his luck in town, but this time he'd preferred to go to bed.

He lay there without moving, staring at the ceiling.

After a moment, she asked if he was sleeping.

She's going to fuck everything up, she said.

He'll realize that soon enough.

But even so, something's ruined. You know it as well as I do, don't pretend otherwise.

Hang on, it's not a done deal yet. What do you think he's got on his mind right now. It must be churning up his brain.

You think so.

We're not just anybody to him.

I can't get over how she jockeyed for position. I don't know if I can keep her on at the shop. I don't know if I can do that.

You should just throw her out, for starters. It would serve her right.

I never thought he'd do this to us. It's really knocked me for a loop. And she knew it, too, she knew what she was doing, and it didn't stop her for a second. She's poisoned my life from day one. Remember what she was like when we first met.

No sense dredging all that up. Come to bed and try to get some sleep.

The next morning, on waking, in the first light of day, Dan contemplated the nude woman sleeping next to him, her clothes on a chair, her glasses on the bedside table. He felt as if he were on a merry-go-round that was spinning faster and faster.

He got dressed for his run. These days, he avoided going near the pond, the lugubrious old wind pump, and cut through a path that passed behind the barracks and skirted the railroad tracks, a much longer route, and so Marlene was in the bathroom when he returned dripping and stinking of sweat, but this inconvenience only annoyed him for a second and he rushed into the kitchen to beat her to the coffee machine. Apart from the disruption, when you started living with someone it set a subtle game in motion, an amusing enough game, constantly filled with twists and turns; if being amused was all you had to do, then living with someone could be rather fun. Living alone could be too, but he felt the poison begin to seep through him and he didn't try to stop it. He put his head under cold water, over the sink, and dried off with two sheets of flowered paper towel.

True, they'd hit a snag, but now that she was here—she'd even brought over a carryall stuffed with her things and she left her phone charger there permanently—there was no turning back. If he didn't

take the plunge now, he never would, he had to fight
or die trying, no other choice. How could Richard and
Nath not understand that. They had completely cracked
up, retreated into their version of the truth, and he didn't
expect to see them for a good long time.

I'm going to talk to them, I'm the one they blame, she
announced.

He had taken his shower and was getting dressed,
listening to Marlene pacing around the house—which
she was rousing from its neurasthenic torpor—until she
came to stand in the bedroom doorway.

We'll go together, he decided. I doubt it'll do any good,
but if you're really set on it, okay.

She's got something to hide. Richard too.

I don't want things to escalate.

Me neither. But I wouldn't hesitate. I'm thinking about
us, first and foremost. I've had it up to here with things
being taken away from me. I say basta, enough.

To end the conversation, she went to sit on his knees
and pulled his arms around her.

The more you have to lose, the stronger you get, she
said. I saw that written on a wall once.

He nodded, mentally echoing, the wronger you get.

He worked on Sundays, his busiest and most tiring
day. You had to keep an eye on everything and expect
the venerable equipment to break down; no time for
daydreaming, wandering in the maze of existential
dilemmas, taking a breather, or lamenting or rejoicing

in your fate. Normally he went on autopilot and waited without waiting for the day to end. Back then, he'd been in no hurry to go home, there was no urgency, nothing crucial to share. But now he discovered that the hours could stretch and slow down even more when you kept watching the clock.

Marlene spent the afternoon preparing her move to Dan's. Not that she was unaware of the dangers of such precipitation, but she sensed she had to act quickly and burn all her bridges. Dan had left her the car and she took advantage to transport her belongings and store them at his place. She hadn't let him in on her plan and only unpacked a portion of it so as not to scare him. Daylight was beginning to wane when she came to the end of her efforts. She sighed, stretched, caressed her belly with a vague smile and took out one last garbage can. It was nice out. She was determined. The sky was empty but she sent up a silent prayer.

Richard knew full well that having sex with Marlene had been a mistake. She was holding a live hand grenade, he had to be careful, it could all blow up in his face if Nath ever learned he'd fucked her sister. He sat at the kitchen table to make his rolls of coins and was down in the dumps. After Mona, now he was losing Dan, it was a shitty Sunday, the only thing missing was rain. He got up to fetch a beer. He couldn't deny that screwing his sister-in-law had had a special tang because of the danger, the taboo attached to it, and anyway you can't change your stripes, he said to himself, they can't hang you for that.

Nath passed in front of him and went to the window. She stood facing the empty street that stretched in either direction from the gate and remained with folded arms before the pale sky with its fading tints. Then she went back to the sofa, leafed through a magazine, and went back to stand at the window. She had been doing this for a while, so he told her to cut it out, that she was making him dizzy.

She shrugged in irritation. I envy you, she said. Just carrying on like everything's fine, like we're not in the middle of a disaster.

Because I look so thrilled, is that it. Maybe you'd like it better if I just paced back and forth.

With the back of his hand, he swept aside the stacks of coins littering the table, sending them flying across the kitchen with a clatter.

She didn't bat an eyelid, not caring whether he broke every dish in the house. Her mind elsewhere, she rubbed a hesitant index finger across her lips, trembling slightly. Marlene knew things. Marlene could unleash chaos at any moment, and it terrified her that her sister had such power. She had forgotten how badly she loathed her in the past, but what was a teenage hatred compared with the hatred of a grown woman whose entire life was at stake, a life patiently built up over twenty years, a herculean effort. No comparison at all. She was finding it hard to breathe. She felt like crying, but she no longer had a single tear to shed.

As the hours went by, Dan had felt an increasing need to be with Marlene, and no longer able to stand it, tired of the surrounding ruckus, he had abandoned his post at the busiest moment to go call her. He had gone outside to the parking lot, where the excess cars spilling into the service roads were causing a real mess. The sun was setting, a slight fog began forming at the foot of the low cliffs bordering the horizon, and behind him the forest was ablaze. He looked at his phone and wondered what to say to her. He couldn't just say he was looking forward to coming home and leave it at that. He looked skyward, seeking inspiration.

Tell her I'm thinking of her. Tell her that despite everything I'm pleased with what's happening to us.

Call her my baby, my darling. He smiled at all that pablum. Tell her you know, I think I'm the one responsible for Mona's death, but small chance of that, it was a secret he'd take with him to the grave.

He put his phone away and resumed work after washing his hands and being grossed out by the filthy hand towel used by the staff—he'd fought in vain to get a hand dryer and he preferred to dry himself on his thighs and butt. Whatever the case, he had no intention of putting in overtime, not an extra minute. Brigitte could shove it up her ass. He was going home. He would pause for a moment, leather jacket in hand, before the empty space where his coat-rack with the duck's head used to stand, and all would be well.

Marlene arrived at her sister's gate at dusk. Over the hedge, she could see Richard in the kitchen and Nath pacing from room to room, arms folded. A few lights shone in the surrounding windows; the neighborhood was deserted, silent. She wondered whether she should ring or use the door code to enter directly. She rang. She said into the intercom that she wanted to come in. Go to hell, Richard answered. You go straight to hell.

The wind had risen again, the eucalyptus leaves clacked against each other. So that's how it was going to be. Anyway, she wasn't really surprised, she'd figured they would be in that state of mind. She rang again for form's sake. She saw their agitated movements inside. She found a rock and flung it at their window. The sound of breaking glass echoed and hung in the air.

Richard and Nath stared at each other, dumbstruck.

I didn't come here to talk, Marlene shouted. Stop trying to turn Dan against me. Just stop it.

Richard and Nath exchanged a few words. Then he disappeared for an instant and reappeared at the front door, which he'd yanked open. He charged across the yard like a buffalo, head lowered, under the eyes of Nath who remained silent, undecided, as he rushed toward the gate.

You take one more step, Richard, and I'll tell her everything, Marlene warned him in a dull voice. It's you, the two of you, who were the bad influence. So just fuck off and leave us alone.

He had already set one foot on the sidewalk but he stopped dead. What's she saying, Nath nervously asked from the window. Richard, what's she telling you.

And you, shut the fuck up, Marlene turned to her. I've had enough of you.

Richard seemed a little drunk but he grabbed her by the arm. She shook free.

Don't touch me. You're monsters, both of you, that's all you are. Dan doesn't know, but I do.

Fuck you, you're just a goddam troublemaker.

I could be worse than that.

Don't listen to her, Richard, make her shut up, Nath yelled. She's trying to destroy us, can't you see that.

Dusk was falling, a neighbor was standing behind his curtains, a night bird hovering in a circle above the woods plunged toward the leafy canopy while Nath let out a bellow of rage and vanished from the window. This is driving us crazy, Marlene shouted, shaking her head. You're both driving me crazy, do you hear.

She turned toward Nath, who strode rapidly over the lawn and emptied the shotgun straight into her chest.

Dan raised his eyes to the bronze sky and let out a long sigh of satisfaction. Brigitte hadn't gotten him this time. He'd stood up to her, taking as his excuse that he had to look after his sick mother, that he couldn't stay any longer, and although she hadn't believed a word of it, she had to give in when he threatened to talk to his union rep.

He straddled his motorcycle and smoked a cigarette before starting up. The early evening was warm, the air smelled new. When he arrived at his door, he ran into the dentist, who was watering his flowers.

Dan, he said, come over here a minute, I wanted to tell you, I think there's a woman who's been living at your place for a few days.

Yes, absolutely, you've got good eyesight. She's not walking around in the buff, I hope.

No, of course not, I never said that.

Because she's kind of like that, you know. But whatever, she does what she likes. She's a bit of a free spirit. You'll get used to her.

Without further ado, he turned and went into his house, addressed a slight smile to the ghost of the coat-rack, and dropped his jacket on a chair. Marlene wasn't home. He glanced into the bedroom and noticed that her things had been put away. He even found a few more, a large suitcase and some cardboard boxes that she had neatly lined up against the garage wall. The hint of a smile came over him. He went back into the kitchen to pour himself a drink. Night was coming on. He sat on the floor, on the cushions in the living room, and relaxed in the uncertain dusk. It just might work. He would tell her that when she got home. Hmm, you and me, I think it could work out. Glad you'll be here.